THE STRAY DOGS

Treadwell Supernatural Directive Book One

ORLANDO A. SANCHEZ

BITTEN PEACHES

ABOUT THE STORY

Some laws are meant to be bent, some ignored, and some...are meant to be shattered.

In mage society, there are laws and those willing to break them.

When laws can no longer be enforced, when there's no hope, there's only one answer.

The Treadwell Supernatural Directive.

Unofficially known as The Stray Dogs, Sebastian Treadwell and his group of operatives will step into the dark corners of the magical underworld, dealing with those who believe themselves untouchable.

When a young mage is killed by Umbra—an organization of dark mages intent on stripping mages of their power—the Stray Dogs are the only group willing to stand against them.

Now Sebastian, together with the Directive, will step into a world other mages fear to face. They will uncover the darkness that feeds off the corruption of power, exposing it to the light and the jaws of justice.

Once the Stray Dogs are on a mission they are relentless —even if the cost is their lives.

Far more violence has been done in obeying the law than in breaking the law.
–Robert Frost

Everyone is a villain in someone's story.
–Unknown

DEDICATION

For those who uphold justice and the law, and know the difference between the two.

ONE

I looked at my second-in-command.

Tiger stared back at me with rage and anguish in her eyes before looking away into the night.

"This was not your fault," I said, trying to console her. "How could you have known?"

"I was just like her at her age," Tiger replied, the pain crushing the words in her chest. "That could've easily been me."

I nodded.

There were no words to answer her. Tiger would forever see herself in every abandoned child, every broken victim. It was what made her, *her*. There was no changing that, so I had learned to accept it, and her, as she was.

It didn't matter that she wielded an immense amount of power, or that she had over the years become one of the most fearsome mages ever to walk the streets of this, or any city, striking fear in her enemies at the mere mention of her name.

A part of her would always be that hungry and lost little girl who nearly died on the streets.

I glanced around the deserted street as the city thrummed

around us, uncaring and unfeeling. East Harlem was rarely quiet at night, but this street was unnaturally silent. Despite the hardness of the city, the block we stood on felt subdued, as if paying its silent respects to the young woman who lay broken and lifeless before us.

I crouched down to get a better look at the victim.

Her dead eyes stared up at me.

She was beautiful in an innocent sort of way—the way all young people possess the inner beauty of youth, with the promise of a life ahead of them.

Not for her, though.

Her life had been snuffed out and stolen.

The anger rose in my chest.

I took a deep breath and composed myself. It would serve no purpose to lose control. No, the control must be maintained, until it was time to unleash death.

"Who found her?" I asked, keeping my voice even for Tiger. "Is this the original crime scene?"

The absence of any authorities struck me as odd.

"Doubt it," Tiger said. "She was discovered by one NYTF Officer Andrews. Rookie's first night out on patrol."

"Rough first night," I said, looking around. "Why are we here alone? Why isn't this scene crawling with NYTF or at the very least, some kind of forensics personnel?"

"Someone with influence tagged her ELP," she said an edge of rage in her voice. "Ramirez disagreed and called me. I called you. This is so far off the books, it doesn't exist."

ELP—Expendable Low Priority—it was the classification used to make someone disappear with minimal involvement from the authorities. At some point tonight, an unmarked vehicle would come and collect the body, storing it in the morgue and labeling it as another Jane Doe. She would effectively disappear in a sea of bureaucracy, her real identity lost, just another victim of the cold city.

By Ramirez calling us, he had prevented her from disappearing. He knew we wouldn't let this go. We would find out who she was, and bring justice to those responsible, no matter how high up the food chain they were.

We were treading into dangerous territory.

"Call Ox and get a vehicle to pick her up."

"Already en route," Tiger said. "Ten minutes."

I nodded, still looking at the woman.

"She's too well-dressed to be homeless," I said, examining her designer clothing. "Escort?"

"Sent the fingerprints to the Church," Tiger said. "Rat is working up a profile, but I don't think so."

"They left her prints," I said, noticing her fingers were intact. "That was either sloppy or a message."

"I'm leaning toward message," she said. "They think they're untouchable. I'm going to show them how wrong they are."

"One thing at a time," I said, keeping calm. "There will be plenty of time for wholesale slaughter later. Right now, we don't even know who the players are."

"But you're going to *see* into it, aren't you?"

I nodded. She knew me too well.

"And the officer in question—this Officer Andrews?" I asked. "Where is he, currently?"

"Out on sick leave for the foreseeable future," she said. "He can't be reached and mysteriously, no one knows where he is."

"Not even Ramirez?"

"*No one*," she said. "It's like he's on leave on another planet."

"If he's still alive, that is," I said. "Someone is eager to make this appear like something it isn't."

"Why not dispose of the body?" Tiger asked. "Makes no sense to leave her here like this. Like trash in the street."

"Same reason they left the prints."

"That doesn't make sense either," she said. "Explain it to me, using small words."

"Makes perfect sense when you think about it," I answered, getting to my feet. "Disposing of the body is an unspoken admission of guilt, so is dissolving her prints. This way, it looks like this young woman wandered into the wrong area at the wrong time, and met an unfortunate end from the locals. Plausible deniability."

"That's bullshit," she spat. "She was murdered."

I raised an eyebrow.

"You have proof of this?"

"Look at her," Tiger said, pointing at the woman.

"I don't see any signs of struggle or wounds," I said, gazing down at the unfortunate woman. "What was the cause of death?"

"Why don't you tell me?" she asked. "*Look* at her."

I removed my glasses and humored her, partly because I was curious and partly because there was no reasoning with her when she was in this state. I learned long ago how to pick my battles with Tiger. This was not a fight I could or would win. She wanted blood, and she would get it one way or another.

I would either help her find out who was responsible for this woman's death, or I would have to get out of her way.

I removed my glasses and looked at the woman.

Once I removed my glasses, my inner sight exploded with trails of energy. I looked down at the woman's body and realized immediately that Tiger was right. The body was devoid of an energy signature. She had been completely drained of life-force.

"You're right," I said, my voice grim. "She's been—"

"Siphoned," Tiger finished. "Someone or something siphoned her dry, which means she was—"

I really hoped it was a 'someone', but I kept that thought to myself.

"She was a mage," I said, now seeing some of the pieces of this puzzle fall into place. "Do we know which affiliation, if any?"

"Don't know yet," Tiger said, frustration clear in her voice. "We're reaching out to the Councils to see if they know anything."

"If she belonged to either of the Councils, they'd be here. She must have been *ronin*—unaffiliated," I said. "That's a risky status to hold these days. Seems like she crossed someone dangerous and powerful. Do we know anyone with a siphoning ability?"

"Inherently or through the use of external devices?"

"Either."

"Inherently—the few mages who possess the ability to siphon life-force are out of the country," she said. "Those who possess an external device or weapon that facilitates a siphon have been located, and a list compiled."

"How many are on that list?"

"Six, so far," she said. "We're still working on it."

"Anyone we know on that list?"

"Two," she said. "Strong, and Stryder the Night Warden. Both possess blades capable of doing this."

"I don't see either of them doing this," I said. "They may have the means, but lack the motive. Narrow down the list to individuals in our world. Search the shadows. Someone knows something, we just have to ask the wrong people the right questions. Start in the Dungeon."

"What? Now?"

"No time like the present," I said, looking at my watch. "They should be open by now. If you hurry, you can catch Char before the evening rush."

The sooner I got her away from the scene, the sooner I could locate who transported the body to this location.

"You know I hate talking with her."

"She's the best information broker in the city," I said. "The only reason you two don't get along is because you're so similar."

A low growl escaped Tiger's throat. It was my *thin ice and cracking* warning.

"If you compare me to that dragon again, you'll be walking funny for a month."

"Understood," I said, raising a hand in surrender. "Go speak to Char, and try to refrain from violence. If anyone knows anything, Char knows which tree to shake."

She nodded.

"What are you going to do?"

"Me? I'm going to find out where she died and see where that takes me."

"You call me first, before taking any action," she said. "I'm serious, Seb. Do not engage whoever did this without me present."

I hated when she called me that and she knew it, which was probably why she did it regularly.

"I'll do my best," I said. "As soon as I find anything of worth, I'll let you know. Call me as soon as you're done with Char. Try not to antagonize her."

"I make no promises," Tiger said. "She can be a right bitch when she wants to be."

"You mean, 'Dragon'?" I said. "It comes with the territory. It's not like you can't hold your own against her."

She smiled.

It was a terrible and frightening thing to see.

"Try not to get dead."

"Not on the agenda for the evening," I said. "Let me know if you discover anything interesting in the Dungeon."

"Will do," she said, walking away. "Watch your back."

"Always," I said to the empty street. She had the unpleasant habit of subtle teleportation and enjoyed flaunting her ability. "Show off."

I turned back to the task at hand.

TWO

I let my gaze go soft, and focused on the area surrounding the woman's body.

I had never subscribed to the whole *narrowing your eyes* method of spectrum shifting. It made mages look ridiculous —like senior citizens losing their sight, and in need of some strong prescription lenses. It was either that, or they tried to appear smoldering and mysterious, which was worse.

One of my abilities, my inner sight, worked in the opposite direction. Instead of having to access it by narrowing my vision, I needed to wear specially runed glasses to control it.

For me, my inner sight was always active.

I examined the street.

The woman may have been missing her energy signature, but she didn't just appear here; someone had brought her body here recently.

Which meant I had a trail to follow.

Energy signatures leave traces.

I realized early on that I could see the traces for much longer than most mages. For most mages, energy signatures were visible in the moment and dissipated shortly after examination.

Accomplished and powerful mages could see the faint traces after three to five minutes, if they were exceptional.

I could see them even after thirty minutes of release. The more traumatic the event, the longer I could see the traces. Once, after a particular horrific death, I could still see the traces after an hour.

I didn't sleep for weeks after that particular operation.

I shook the memory away with a shudder, and focused on the traces around her body. None of them were hers, but they were closely linked to her. Whoever had brought her body here had been agitated and was fairly strong in ability. The traces led me out of the street I currently stood in.

I walked back to her body and waited.

Several minutes later, a large black van pulled up.

It stopped close to her body; the driver cut the headlights and exited the vehicle, which swayed to and fro as he stepped out.

"Ox," I said with a nod. "Thank you for coming."

He was dressed in his usual gray suit version of a mageiform. He didn't favor the black most mages wore. His white shirt was accented by a dark gray tie with ivory accents down its length.

"Sure thing, Boss," he said, looking around the street. "Not the best of neighborhoods. Are you looking for a fight?"

"Not particularly," I said. "She's the reason I'm here."

I pointed at the woman.

"Tiger mentioned a body," he said, looking down at the woman. "Jane Doe?"

"For now," I said, as he lifted the body effortlessly and placed her gently in the back of the van, which held a modified gurney for occasions like this. "Rat should have information on her by the time you get back."

"You on the hunt?"

"It was me or Tiger," I said. "I sent her to the Dungeon to get information. Having her loose on the streets would have been...bloody."

"You better hope she doesn't piss off Char," Ox said, securing the body in the gurney. "That can be just as bloody."

"At least it will be contained to one location," I said. "Char will let Tiger vent and deal with her. I needed Tiger off the streets for this. You recall the last time?"

"*Everyone* recalls the last time," Ox said. "We needed most of the Directive to bring her in. Even then, it was dicey."

I nodded.

"She *can* be a force to be reckoned with," I said. "Call me when you get back. I have a trail to follow."

"Will do," he said. "Is this an S&D?"

"I don't know yet," I said. "It's too early to call it a Seek and Destroy op, but she *was* siphoned. I need to know how, why, and by whom."

"Siphoned?" he said. "You don't see that everyday."

"No, no you don't."

He jumped in the van, started the engine, and turned on the headlights a second later.

"You know where to find me," he said. "Give me a call if it turns out to be more than you bargained for. Watch your six."

"Certainly," I said with a nod as the van pulled away. "Drive safe."

He nodded and sped off.

I turned to follow the faint energy signature trail.

THREE

The trail led me farther uptown, into territory I knew and usually avoided.

This was the stomping ground of the renegades and *ronin* —mages that served no one but themselves, and killed for the ability to do so.

Even the Councils avoided entering this territory unless absolutely necessary, and then only with overwhelming numbers and force.

I was walking in here alone and hunting a potential murderer.

Not the best of scenarios, but it couldn't be helped.

I was not a hero.

I had made peace with that fact.

A hero would sacrifice you to save the world. A villain would sacrifice the world to save you. Some would call that heartless and cruel.

Me? I called it pragmatic.

It didn't mean I would look the other way when someone was murdered, especially after Ramirez had gone out of his way to get me involved.

There was more here.

There were entities involved that the NYTF couldn't touch: powerful people who were used to acting with impunity, escaping the consequences of their actions.

No one escaped us.

"What do we have here?" a voice said from across the street. "This stray looks lost. What do you think, Bobby?"

I had seen the two sentries pretending to loiter on the street, and knew they would approach once I got too close. They were both young, thin, wiry men, with low energy signatures. They didn't pose a threat as mages, but I was certain they could be loud and get attention.

Attention I didn't want.

Their energy signatures didn't match the one I was tracking, so I was willing to let them continue their evening without violence.

They had other plans.

"I don't know, Anton." I could only assume it was Bobby who answered. "Maybe we should help him back downtown? You lost, stray?"

"I'm looking for someone," I said. "Someone dangerous."

"Ooh, aren't we all?" Bobby said and thought himself amusing as he laughed at his response. He grew serious a moment later. "You're in the wrong neighborhood to be looking for anything, except a quick exit from this life. Are you looking to die, old man?"

"I don't want any trouble—"

"Then you should've stayed home," Anton said, drawing a short knife and stepping closer. "That's the problem with trouble—even when you aren't looking for it, sometimes it's looking for you."

I took a few steps back and assessed the situation.

I noticed most of the vehicles on the street were normal

modes of transport, except for three, black rune-covered cargo vans parked one behind the other.

They weren't SuNaTran. The runes were unfamiliar and too rudimentary to be Cecil's work. These vans probably belonged to one of the groups in the area. I filed the runes I could see on the sides away for future reference.

If I took the time to end them, it would slow my pursuit. I could lose the energy signature trail, and then I would have to resort to more conventional methods of gathering information, methods that would attract unwanted and unneeded attention.

If I ignored them, they would interpret my reluctance to attack as weakness and engage me, resulting in their injury or death, taking me back to square one.

When tact and diplomacy failed, bribery was always an available alternative, except, considering where I was, flashing large amounts of cash would have the same result as chum in shark-infested waters—a bad idea.

Still, I had no desire to shed blood tonight, at least not theirs, but it couldn't be helped. I would have to opt for the path of least resistance and most effectiveness. Someone would have to become a cautionary tale.

I formed my weapons—twin karambits, small curved knives that resembled claws. They were runed as kamikiras, which meant they were exceptionally lethal and absolutely banned pretty much everywhere.

I still remember Master Yat's words when I chose them as my signature weapon: *These are karambit, they are not elegant. They are ruthless, efficient, and brutal. They are designed to be wielded closer than any other blade. If you choose this weapon, you must become intimate with death, more so with these, than with other blades.*

I had chosen them, or rather as I had told Master Yat, they had chosen me.

I refocused on the sentries and positioned myself between them. I would give them one more opportunity to leave the area unscathed.

"Where exactly am I?" I asked, looking around the street. "It seems I must have gotten myself turned around."

"Lost and clueless," Anton said. "Typical DV—designated victim. You want him, Bobby?"

"No," Bobby said immediately, shaking his head and stepping back. "He smells off. You take him."

"You scared Bobby?" Anton jeered. "Scared of a lost old man? He's just a DV. Let me show you how it's done."

Anton, who still held his drawn blade, closed the distance on me. I stepped back, sliding to the side so that Bobby, if he chose to join the dance, would have to go through Anton to get to me.

"You don't have to do this," I said, moving back. "I can just go back the way I came."

"Too late for that, old man," Anton said. "You stepped into Umbra territory. You made the last mistake of your life."

Umbra territory. I would have to follow up on that later.

I stopped backing up, but made sure I had enough room to maneuver. Anton lunged forward with a thrust.

Too slow.

I stepped to the side, allowing the thrust to pass harmlessly next to me. Before he could withdraw his arm, I sliced at his forearm, leaving a long but shallow wound. I followed that up with several more slashes, working my way across his arm and up his torso as the blades spun in my hands.

Each of the movements was designed to cut, not sever. I didn't want to end his life here, but he would now think twice about attacking strangers.

The last slash was designed to sever his carotid arteries and end his life. I stopped just short of spilling his life on the street, holding one of my blades across his neck, while I placed the point of the other under his chin.

"It's rude to call people old," I whispered into Anton's ear. "Wouldn't you agree?"

He nodded slowly.

I heard Bobby's footsteps recede into the distance as he ran away.

"Don't...don't kill me...please," he pleaded as I remained focused on him. "What do you want?"

"Your partner in crime left you alone," I said, keeping my voice low. "You know what I want?"

"What? What do you want?" he said, panicked. "I don't know what you want!"

"Shh," I let the point of my karambit dig in just under his chin, drawing some blood. He became silent, his eyes widening at the realization of his imminent death. "I want you to give me a reason why I shouldn't leave your cold, dead body on this street. What is Umbra?"

"I'm just eyes on the street," he said. "You don't want to kill me. I'm nobody. You really want Michael, he runs this area for Umbra."

I felt the energy spike and jumped back as a red orb crashed into Anton, impacting his body. He let out one last gasp and I knew he was dead before he fell to the ground.

I absorbed my blades and turned to face this new threat.

"And you run your mouth more than you should, Anton," a voice said from the darkness. I guessed Bobby had gone for reinforcements and had come back with Michael. "Who are you?"

"No one of consequence."

"You're going to tell me, or you're going to die."

"If I were you, I'd start getting used to disappointment."

Michael stepped into the dim light of the street and I

realized in that moment that only one of us was going to walk away from this meeting tonight.

He had the energy signature I was tracking.

FOUR

Michael was a mage.

Not a very powerful mage, but still a threat to be reckoned with. He was dressed in a gray shirt and black slacks. A definite step up from the sentries, but nowhere near the leadership of the group.

At most, he was a glorified foot soldier.

He didn't seem powerful enough to siphon the life-force, but I had learned early on that looks could be deceiving. He may not have been the murderer, but he was certainly involved in transporting and dumping the body.

If he didn't kill the woman, he knew who did.

"You've made a fatal mistake," Michael said, as he shook out his hands. "The last mistake you'll ever make."

"Why?" I asked, raising a hand as he prepared to blast me. "Why kill her and dump her body?"

The question took him off-guard and provided the insight I needed. Definitely lower ranked in the hierarchy of this Umbra. A trained killer wouldn't have hesitated to attack. Michael was operating on a preset group of instructions, probably along the lines of: If anyone comes looking or asking for the woman, take care of them—permanently—no loose ends.

"I didn't kill her."

One question answered.

"But *you* moved the body," I said. "You may as well tell me since it seems my time on this earth is about to be cut short. Consider it a dying man's last wish."

He gave it thought for a few seconds, apparently coming to the conclusion I posed little to no threat.

He nodded to himself, pausing the blast he was about to unleash.

"She pissed off the wrong people," he said dispassionately. "It was a drain and dump. She was getting too close, and sticking her nose in the wrong places; management gave the word and they ended her."

"What were your instructions?"

"Move the body and eliminate anyone who asked the same questions you're asking," he said, cracking his neck. "Time to say goodnight, nothing personal."

"I've always found that when people state it's nothing personal, that it's quite personal for the victim," I said, controlling my anger. "Is that what they told her? It wasn't personal?"

"You ask too many questions, old man."

He released another red orb of death, which I dodged.

An expression of surprise crossed his face.

While rare, dodging orbs wasn't unheard of. I had the added advantage of being able to see the streams of power that formed when energy was being controlled and manipulated. It formed something of an early warning detection system in my mind.

It didn't mean I was prescient, but it gave me a slight

advantage when dealing with mages and those who used energy as a weapon.

"How...how did you?" he asked, before resigning himself to his task. "You move quick for a senior citizen."

He produced a long blade, intent on cutting me down.

"You have no idea," I said, moving forward as I formed one of my blades, sidestepping his thrust, then ducking under a slash designed to remove my head. I buried my blade into his side, just under an armpit. I've heard it called one of the most excruciating wounds. "I have one more question."

"Fuck, you," he managed as he spit up blood. "I'm not telling...telling you...anything."

He fell to one knee, gasping for air.

"I've punctured one of your lungs," I said, my voice cold. "Without my help, you're going to die—not quickly, but certainly. Who drained her? Give me a name, and I'll make sure you live to die another day, on my word."

"Fakul Bijan," he said. "That's all...that's all I know. Never met him, I just do what I'm told. He drained her, and then I got the call to relocate...relocate the body."

It was doubtful he would have any more information, but it wouldn't hurt to ask.

"Where do I find this Fakul?"

Michael shook his head and laughed, or at least attempted to. His laugh was cut off, quickly becoming a series of bloody coughs as he gasped for air.

"You don't find him, he finds you," he said. "You can't face him or Umbra. They're too powerful. Help...help me. You gave your word."

"That I did," I said, forming a small orb that gave off a golden glow. "This will take care of your wound and block access to your sacral nexus."

"What?" he asked. "My sacral what?"

"Means no more energy manipulation for you for the foreseeable future," I said. "Now, hold still."

I released the orb and it floated over to his body. It descended and impacted him in his lower abdomen, covering his body with the same golden glow it held.

Within seconds, his wound was healed.

He slowly got to his feet and stared at me.

"You healed me," he said. "I can't believe it—you healed me?"

"I said I would and so I did," I said with a short nod. "Your body is whole, but you can't cast, at least—"

"You must be truly suicidal," he scoffed. "You healed me."

"As I was saying, I wouldn't try to—"

He tried to form another red orb of death, and spontaneously combusted. Golden flames incinerated him where he stood, reducing him to ash in seconds.

He didn't even have time to scream.

"—to form another orb," I finished. "Bloody hell, they never listen, do they?"

I pulled out my phone and dialed the Church.

"Treadwell Supernatural Directive Headquarters, how may I direct your call?"

"Hello, Rabbit," I said. "Is Rat available?"

"Hello, Boss, he's downstairs in his lab, getting information on that Jane Doe," she said. "Want me to transfer you?"

"Yes, please," I said. "Has Tiger called in?"

"Not yet, but I hear the Dungeon is still standing, so it can't be all bad. One second, transferring you now."

A moment of silence and then a soft-spoken voice.

"Yes?"

"Any progress?"

"I should be getting her information within the hour," Rat said. "But you didn't call for that." He had a way of knowing my intentions without my having to state them. "What am I searching for now?"

"Two things," I said. "A person of interest named Fakul Bijan, and an organization called Umbra. Do either of those sound familiar to you?"

"Bijan does not, but Umbra...hold on one second," he said as I heard the tapping of keys. "Yes, there have been rumors of a new organization of dark mages operating in the city. Something about dwelling in the shadows of the light."

"What makes you think it's this Umbra?"

"Aside from the lack of creativity in the name, you mean?"

"Yes, besides that."

"My informants tell me these dark mages are growing in power by siphoning life-force from young or novice mages," Rat said. "Mages who are unaware of their talents or have just started exhibiting abilities are their prime targets. Our Jane Doe fits the description."

"Can you corroborate this activity near my location?"

I waited for a few more seconds as he located me.

"The siphoning activity seems to be citywide, but there are some clusters near your location," he said. "My educated guess is that this Umbra and the new group of dark mages are one and the same."

"Find out who this Fakul is, and where they're headquartered," I said. "I need to go see a dragon."

"Char?"

"Yes, Char."

"I'd advise you to be careful, but you know that already," he said. "Give her my regards."

"I will," I said. "Call me as soon as we have a positive ID on the Jane Doe."

"I'll send over the information as soon as I have it," he said. "Is Tiger with you?"

"She's at the Dungeon, I sent her on ahead."

"I see," he said. "I'll make sure the rest of the team is on heightened alert, in case we need to extricate her from there."

"Not an entirely bad idea," I admitted. "Speak soon."

I ended the call and headed downtown to speak to a dragon.

FIVE

The Dungeon was designed to turn people away.

If you knew of its existence.

The first obstacle, was actually finding it. Not everyone who knew of the Dungeon, knew where it was located. Char took a sadistic delight in having the Dungeon shift location every few days.

The only way to find the Dungeon after a location shift was to know the rotation of locales Char used. Those, at least, were fixed—even if the Dungeon itself was not.

There were several ways to know which of the five locales was being used currently; approaching any of them uninvited could prove fatal, and only one method worked without fail. The foolproof method was to call the Dungeon—if you could somehow miraculously acquire the number, which was almost as difficult to obtain as the knowledge of the Dungeon itself.

If you managed to get the number—which only Char knew and dispensed at her pleasure—you would need to know when to call. Calls would only be answered for one minute each hour. At exactly half-past any hour, a call could be made and would be answered with a location.

One minute past half, and the line would go dead, only to be active again the next hour, for exactly one minute.

I once asked Char why all the mystery and intrigue, when she could have simply made her lounge inaccessible and planted several intimidating and powerful personnel at the entrance, thus ensuring limited access.

She smiled and shook her head.

I remembered her words:

Where's the fun in that, Bas?

She was the only living being allowed to call me by that nickname. There was a very good reason for this: aside from the fact that she was ancient—and I respected my elders—she *was* a dragon.

She could call me anything she wanted.

Everyone wants to feel special and unique. They want to belong to something exclusive and— more importantly in our world— forbidden. The Dungeon provides that. I provide that. My clientele understand that to enter my domain, my home, is a rare privilege, not a right, and appreciate the opportunity to do so. Wouldn't you agree?

I agreed.

Personally, the Dungeon held no allure for me. It never had. It was important however, because through the Dungeon, I had access to Char. Information was power and that made Char one of the most powerful beings in the city.

If I had a question, Char usually had the answer; if she didn't, she knew who did. As long as the cost was met, you could have the answer to any question you presented to her.

If you failed to meet her cost, you would be indebted to her.

You never wanted to be indebted to a dragon.

Especially when that dragon was Char.

I arrived at the downtown location of the Dungeon.

Char and I had history, which meant I was one of the few individuals who received daily alerts of its location. Uptown, downtown, west, east, or Central Park were the five locations it shifted to, in that rotation.

I preferred the downtown location due to its convenience and proximity to the Church, and its selection of venue. This location of the Dungeon occupied the space beneath 215 Centre Street in the heart of Chinatown.

Beside the entrance to MOCA—the Museum of Chinese Americans—stood a nondescript, gray, double door. In front of this door, stood two very unassuming but dangerous individuals—one male, one female.

No matter where the Dungeon was located, these two were always at the front door—Fuxi and Nuwa.

They were known as the Twins of Death.

They both wore impeccable Brioni Midnight Blue suits, offset with rose-colored shirts. Fuxi wore a blood red tie and Nuwa wore a cravat of the same color. Nuwa wore her hair long, while Fuxi kept his short.

Their porcelain white skin nearly shone in the night as I approached the door. Both gave me a short nod as I placed a hand on the runes next to the entrance.

The entrance runes served a dual purpose, they would announce my presence to Char and identify that it was truly me and not an impostor trying to access the Dungeon.

"Mr. Treadwell," Fuxi said when the runes flashed a deep blue. "Welcome to the Dungeon. I trust you have been well?"

"As well as can be expected," I said. "Has Tiger needed your attention?"

Nuwa smiled and shook her head.

"She has been uncharacteristically subdued this evening," Nuwa said. "Is she feeling ill?"

"She must be distracted," I replied, thankful Tiger had restrained herself. "I doubt she is ill."

"It has been...quiet," Fuxi said. "A welcome change."

"One I'm afraid will be short lived if I know Tiger," I said.

"Would you be so kind as to contact Ox and have the Tank delivered here?"

"Of course," Nuwa said with a slight bow. "Your vehicle will be waiting for you upon your exit from the Dungeon. Will there be anything else?"

"Is Lady Char available?"

"For you, always," Nuwa replied. "She has been notified of your arrival and is waiting downstairs...with Tiger."

Char was *always* on the premises, but this was part of our ritual. It was also another part of the vetting process. Every guest of the Dungeon was required to inquire if Char was available. Failure to do so would ensure you would be asked to leave the premises, violently if necessary.

"Lady Char is in and expecting you," Fuxi said. "Please observe the customs of our home and enjoy your visit to the Dungeon."

I nodded and stepped forward as the gray doors slid open, revealing a staircase leading down. The customs of the Dungeon were encapsulated in one rule.

No violence or know pain.

The Dungeon was considered a neutral zone of sorts.

It didn't mean violence wasn't possible. I had witnessed plenty of deaths within the walls of the Dungeon. The victims were usually the ones who had broken the rule.

I took the stairs down.

The smell of citrus, lavender, and a hint of cinnamon was the first thing I noticed. The low sounds of jazz played as the backdrop to the sound of subdued conversations, creating a symphony of speech and music.

The reception area was designed as a large lounge. I nick-named it the Area of the Beautiful People. It was the space where people came to see and be seen. Comfortable seating, large sofas, and oversized wingbacks around small tables provided the guests plenty of opportunities to gaze upon the evening's visitors.

I looked around the floor, sensing the energy signatures of several of the guests. Most of them were here to impress. Several were major contenders vying for control, but a handful wielded real power, preferring to remain in the shadows of the lounge and occupying the spaces away from the center of the floor.

In the center of the floor was a large oval-shaped bar catering to the requests of the guests, and in the center of that bar, I saw Wu Wei, the head of security for the entire Dungeon, leaning casually against its side.

His casual demeanor disguised one of the most fearsome combat mages I had ever seen in action. The only mage capable of giving him a run for his money was the fearsome force of nature I knew as my second, Tiger.

The last time Tiger had lost it in the Dungeon, Wei had ended up in Haven, with multiple breaks and injuries, forcing Char to step in personally. The only reason he hadn't retaliated with a death hunt—aside from Char prohibiting it—was because the injuries were incurred in battle and Tiger was fearsome.

For him, it was a badge of honor to survive her attack. I had a feeling he was eagerly awaiting round two.

I stepped up to the bar, giving him a slight nod.

"Lemon water for Mr. Treadwell," Wu said to the bartender, before turning to face me. "What's wrong with Tiger?"

"I don't understand," I said, concerned. "What do you mean, what's wrong?"

"She's been here at least thirty minutes, and nothing is destroyed," Wu said with a smile. "Then she asked Lady Char for a conversation. Is she looking to die tonight? Even *I* don't ask Lady Char for conversations, not unless I wish to recover in Haven."

I sighed in quiet relief. At least Tiger had directed her rage in the best possible direction. Char could deal with whatever Tiger unleashed.

"She's still processing the events of this evening," I said. "Where's Char?"

"Downstairs. They should be in the middle of their *conversation* right about now."

"Char agreed?"

Wu nodded, and then shook his head.

"I know she's formidable, but Lady Char is beyond her ability," Wu said. "Tiger is going to get her ass handed to her —painfully. What happened?"

"I'll explain later," I said, taking my lemon water. "I'm heading downstairs. Maybe I can prevent a visit to Haven tonight."

"Good luck," he said, with another nod. "Let me know how that goes."

I returned the nod and navigated my way around the lounge heading towards the door that led downstairs. In front of this door stood a human wall of destruction known as Bam-Bam, one of Wu's security personnel.

He was easily as large as Ox and probably just as dangerous. I could barely make out the door frame behind his immense bulk. Bam-Bam looked over and caught Wu's eye, who nodded.

Bam-Bam stepped to the side and gave me a short nod.

To my knowledge, Bam-Bam never spoke, unless it was with his fists—and he was incredibly proficient in the language of pain.

I proceeded to head downstairs.

SIX

The stairs were covered in runes as I made my way down.

I paused on the final step and took a deep breath.

The smell shifted here, and the scent transported me to an open forest full of trees with a gentle wind blowing. The faint scent wafted into my lungs, carrying hints of vanilla, rose, and lilac, reminding me of cherry blossoms.

How Char managed to pull this off always astounded me. It wasn't a similarity; if I closed my eyes and paused for a second, I could swear I was standing in a forest. It was some kind of sensory cast that spoke to the power that Char wielded.

I took a moment to refocus on the steps, making sure the runes etched into the stone were set to defense and not active offense. Even though I knew she expected me, it never hurt to make sure. Char was known for keeping her guests on their toes. Each of the runes I observed was defensive in nature, capable of stopping everything—short of a horde of angry ogres charging down the stairs.

For that, there was the set of glowing runes at the threshold of the training area.

The actual horde of ogres that had attacked long ago, sent here by one of Char's ancient enemies, *were* stopped dead in their tracks—quite literally—by the glowing annihilation runes around the circular training area situated in the center of the training floor.

It must have come as quite a surprise—to the ogres especially. From what I later gathered, a magnified variation of the runes containing a potent combination of obliteration and oblivion runes, had blasted the ogres from existence the moment they attempted to cross the threshold.

Never attack a dragon in their lair—it's not conducive to a long life.

I checked the annihilation runes and, thankfully, they were deactivated from active destruction. In their current state, a trespasser would suffer a nasty jolt and probably wake up a few days later, wondering what had happened.

I paused, again, at the foot of the stairs and let my eyes adjust to the low lighting as I examined the space.

This entire sub-level was easily three times the size of the level above us. It was divided into two sections, with a clear delineation between the two, one area for training, which dominated the center of the floor, and the other for negotiations. The training area was comprised of defined sections for sparring and fighting—two very distinct expressions of combat I learned as a young mage—with each area catering to different disciplines.

Many disputes that were resolved in Char's training area, if left to their natural course, would have resulted in a minor war on the streets of the city.

It wasn't so much a neutral zone as it was a resolution zone. If there was an enemy you needed to confront, you invited them for a conversation at Char's.

It was poor form to refuse such an invitation, and almost

always viewed as weakness, prompting direct attacks. Using Char's location as a conflict resolution zone was the preferred method of preventing wholesale slaughter on the streets in the world I inhabited.

It was efficient, effective, and ruthless.

Very much like Char herself.

The negotiation area was behind a transparent, floor-to-ceiling wall of plexan. A large, black marble conference table dominated that space.

Thirteen chairs sat around the table.

All of the chairs were black—the only exception being Char's, which was a bone white, ornately engraved seat, resembling a throne more than an executive chair.

In all my visits to the Dungeon, I had never seen the negotiation area being used. Currently, it was closed, the dim lighting in the space shining off the large, marble table.

Char had once explained that more blood had been shed around that table than had ever been spilled on the training floor.

I had no doubt.

With a word, she could wipe out entire factions in the city. One did not cross Char and expect to live long. On the other hand, if you possessed a powerful death wish—the non-caffeine kind—it was a spectacular way to end your existence. At the very least it would be memorable.

I brought my focus back to the two figures in the center of the training circle. The old wood of the circle had been polished to a high sheen, and the deadly runes around the circle pulsed a bright green warning every few seconds.

No one was getting in that circle until Char wanted them to.

"I'll be right with you, Bas," Char said, never taking her eyes off Tiger. "Tiger and I are almost done."

"Don't rush on my account," I said, taking a seat on one of the nearby benches. "How goes the *conversation*?"

"Constructive," Tiger said with a growl as she focused on Char. "Lady Char is just explaining why going out and eviscerating whoever killed that girl was a bad idea."

Char gave her a nod with a slight smile.

Tiger towered over Char who stood a few inches below five feet. Like Fuxi and Nuwa, Char's skin was porcelain white, but unlike the two at the front door, her skin actually gave off a subtle, white glow of inherent power.

Char always came across as unassuming. She presented herself as an elderly woman, but I had seen her shift into a beautiful young woman, and once even as a young man.

I figured her true form was that of a dragon, but she seemed to prefer the guise of the elderly woman. It had a dual effect. It made people inherently trust her; she gave off a definite grandmother feel. For others it made them underestimate her.

I had seen her toss several of her security like dolls while in this guise. She may have looked elderly, but she wielded the power of an ancient dragon.

I had never seen her in her dragon form, and frankly, I didn't think I ever wanted to. From what I had been told, her creature form was a fabled, white dragon that struck fear in all those who gazed upon her.

I don't remember if anyone who had seen her in that form had survived the encounter. It was not something I was looking forward to experiencing in my lifetime.

Currently, she was wearing a simple, gray robe with a repeating white dragon in flight motif. Her long, white hair was pulled back into a bun and held in place with several long, silver hairpins.

The fact that she entertained Tiger's moments of rage

always baffled me. I wondered if Char saw something of herself in the much younger Tiger. I had no explanation for it. Char didn't suffer fools gladly, and Tiger, though prone to mindnumbing acts of violence, was anything but foolish. However, Char would allow Tiger free access to the Dungeon whenever she wanted to go on a rampage.

I had never understood their relationship, except to surmise that they were cut from the same cloth—not that I would ever admit that out loud in front of Char.

If Tiger was touchy on the subject, Char was verifiably lethal on being compared to anyone that wasn't another dragon. Even then, it was safer to refrain from making any type of comparison. It would be safer measuring her up against forces of nature, like a category 5 hurricane or an megaquake that registered a 10 on the Richter scale, than to another living being.

"Rage and vengeance are like fire," Char said in her clear, melodic voice as she focused on Tiger. "Controlled—they are useful weapons. Unleashed without thought or purpose—you are more likely to destroy yourself than your enemy."

Tiger let out a slow, controlled breath. Outwardly she looked calm; inside she was seething. This rage she held wasn't directed at Char. If it had a target, it would be those who harmed the weak, those with power who would exert it just because they could.

She had a particular brand of righteous indignation. I had stopped trying to understand it long ago. Our last discussion on the subject ended with several thousands of dollars of destroyed property.

I had once suggested she join the Light Council since she felt so principled about the wielding of power and helping out those who were weak. She had offered a counter-suggestion of pain in exponential quantities.

It went downhill from there.

"Right now, all I feel like doing is ripping some enemies to shreds," Tiger said and then looked at me. "I hope you brought me some good news."

"Depends on what you consider to be good news," I said, waving her on to continue her conversation with Char. "But, don't mind me. We can talk after you get this out of your system."

"It will never get out of my system," she said with her signature low growl. "This just keeps the rage at bay for a time."

I nodded.

"By all means, unleash."

Tiger refocused on Char and attacked.

There were reasons Tiger was so feared.

As a mage, her discipline made her what was often called a 'knocker', not that I would ever call her *that* to her face; she hated that nickname for her discipline. In her case, her mastery of the kinetic arts surpassed the understanding of most mages.

Even mine.

Tiger had honed her skill to such a degree that she could harness the internal movements of her body into kinetic energy. She was a potential threat as long as her heart was beating. If she was able to blink or even move a finger, she could harness the kinetic energy in her body, using it as a weapon.

Any motion was potential energy to be exploited. She embodied the old Chinese proverb: *The flapping wings of a butterfly can be felt on the other side of the world.* This defined Tiger's ability—as long as that flapping resulted in devastating destruction.

In addition to her kinetic power, she had mastered body hardening, and possessed accelerated healing. By redirecting the kinetic energy into a shield, she could withstand practically any physical attack and heal nearly instantly from those that managed to get through her defenses.

I had witnessed her take a full-on blow from an infuriated ogre and return the favor, launching said ogre across a street, into a building and cratering a wall.

Her weaknesses lay in magical attacks. Kinetic mages had difficulty dealing with energy attacks. Even though Tiger was making progress in that area, her discipline didn't allow for the casting of orbs, not in the conventional sense.

I truly hoped she would never master energy manipulation. The time she had lost control, it took most of the Directive to bring her back to her senses without doing lasting damage.

I knew that if I ever had to stop her by myself, I could. It would be a bloody and painful process; but I could, if I had to. Whether we would both survive such an encounter was uncertain, which was why I took measures to never let it occur.

This was one of the reasons I sent her regularly to Char.

Her volatility notwithstanding, Tiger was one of the few on the planet I would want by my side, if I was in a fight for survival.

I trusted Tiger with my life.

I took another sip of lemon water, and executed one of my favorite casts, converting the sour liquid to bitter caffeine goodness. The aroma of potent coffee quickly filled the training area.

Char glanced at me and rolled her eyes with a shake of her head. She turned back to Tiger and beckoned to her with her hand.

"Get on with it, child," she said. "I'm not getting younger while you find your courage."

Tiger closed the distance and unleashed several attacks at

Char. Tiger, like me, preferred to fight at close quarters; unlike me, she used her own variation on an ancient martial art called Bagua.

Her attacks were circular in nature. Where I would proceed in a linear fashion, closing the distance in the quickest method possible, Tiger would close and immediately move off center, stepping in a circular way.

It was an infuriating style to fight against, mostly made that way by her constant comments. Comments she refrained from when facing Char.

Char stood still as Tiger closed.

Her hands open, she slid in and unleashed several palm strikes at Char's chest. The latter, pivoting slightly, avoided all of the strikes with twists of her body, using her shoulders to gently nudge Tiger's arm off-target, causing her to miss each time.

Tiger bent low, and raised both arms in a double-handed claw strike, aimed at raking Char's body with her fingers. Using her kinetic ability, I had seen her rake through a steel door with the same ability.

She wasn't holding back.

Char on the other hand, was.

She leaned back just out of reach of Tiger's double upward rake and then immediately leaned in, lightly tapping Tiger on the forehead with a closed fist.

Tiger flew back, crashing into a wall. She rolled off and jumped, aiming the leap to land her back into the center of the circle.

From my few *conversations* with Char, I knew leaving the ground with both feet was a colossal error when facing the dragon. Actually, Tiger knew this as well, but she was what I liked to call 'determinedly focused'.

Char stepped forward and extended a palm.

"What did I tell you about jumping into an attack?" Char

asked softly as she followed the arc of Tiger's jump with her gaze. "You are not a bird, nor do you possess the power of flight."

Before Tiger could land, Char unleashed a blast of bright, white energy from her palm, spinning Tiger in the air, before unleashing a devastating kick to her midsection that sent her flying out of the training circle.

Tiger landed outside the circle with a crash and a groan.

"Ow. You told me...you told me not to," Tiger said, slowly getting to her knees and slipping into a *seiza* position of sitting on her knees. She bowed to Char. "Thank you, Lady Char."

Char returned the bow, walking over to where Tiger lay and extended a hand. Tiger took it and stood.

"You know I hate ceremony," Char said, glancing my way. "You're almost as stubborn as that one. No wonder you two work so well together."

"I'm not stubborn," I countered. "I'm single-minded of purpose."

"Like a starving dog with a bone, the both of you."

"My apologies, Lady Char," Tiger said with another bow. "I'll work on it."

"You let your emotions rule you," Char said, tapping Tiger's forehead with a finger as she scowled. It quickly turned into a small smile as she continued. "Part of this is a product of your youth. The other part is that you are impetuous. You must learn to calm yourself in the heat of battle."

"Yes, Lady Char, thank you," Tiger said, properly chastised. "I will remember."

"Hasn't happened yet," Char said with a smile. "But there's always hope. Go get cleaned up; I have much to discuss with Bas."

Tiger bowed again and gave me a look that said: *you had*

better tell me everything I miss, as she headed to the stairs. I nodded to her and she sped up the stairs.

"Bas," Char said, getting my attention. "You have questions, yes?"

"I do."

We headed to the negotiation area.

SEVEN

Once inside the conference room, Char waved a hand, and the plexan wall became an opaque milky-white, blocking the view from the outside.

She sat in her chair and I waited, standing until she motioned to the chair closest to her, on her right.

"Come, sit," she said. "You have questions and I have news for you."

"News for me?"

That could either be fantastic or horrific. Char had a way of sharing that always gave me pause.

"Do I really want to know this news you have?"

"Ask your questions first, then I will give you your news and a word."

'A word' definitely meant horrific.

I sighed and gathered my thoughts as she smiled at me.

"A woman was siphoned uptown," I started as she leaned back and focused on me. "She was a mage, just coming into her power."

She gestured and materialized a small cup of coffee so black it absorbed the light from the lamps above us. The powerful aroma of coffee filled the conference area. I knew better than to ask for a cup. I had made that error once, and ended up staying awake for a week straight.

The nightmares produced by that singular cup of dragon coffee were exquisitely horrifying, preventing sleep for a few weeks afterwards.

She called it her Death Wish Extreme, but it was unlike any coffee I had ever had. Whatever it was she had created transcended the potency and safety of what I, or most humans, called coffee. She took a sip, but kept her eyes on me. Placing her cup silently on the table, she waited for me to continue.

"I followed the trail uptown, and learned of a new organization of dark mages operating in the city. A group of dark mages calling themselves Umbra."

"What else?" she asked. "There was more, I'm sure."

"Fakul Bijan," I said. "This is the individual who siphoned the girl. Who is he, and what is this Umbra?"

I didn't insult her by asking her if she knew Fakul Bijan or what kind of organization Umbra was.

She knew.

She always knew.

She raised a finger and took another sip from her cup. Her eyes gleamed with a subtle, white flash. Even with her energy signature diminished, she still radiated immense power.

It felt like sitting before a barely controlled explosion of energy—that impressive and that dangerous. It was always this way. Part of me watched her in awe, while the other part advised me that vacating the premises would be the safest course of action and should be taken immediately.

She finished her coffee and the cup slowly vanished from her fingers.

"Before I answer your questions, my news."

I sat back surprised; she rarely refused to answer a question directly. This was unlike her, and concerned me. This news had to be worse than I imagined.

"Your news," I said, treading carefully. Char was not a being to be rushed. "Please, do share."

"Your Shadow Queen is in the city," Char said. "She will reach out to you soon."

"My apologies, but we didn't leave things on the best of terms," I said, remembering the blade in my chest when I last spoke to Regina Clark...the love of my life. I chose my words prudently, feeling my way through this conversation as if wandering lost through a forest full of deadly traps. "I don't believe she will seek me out."

"Are you saying I'm...mistaken?"

"I would never presume to make such a judgment," I said as the temperature in the conference area rose a few degrees. "I'm merely stating that when she and I last spoke, it was less than amicable. She buried one of her blades in my chest. Not an act conducive to productive conversation. I don't see a reason for her to seek me out."

"She doesn't *need* a reason," Char said. "In her own way, she cares for you. In fact, I would say the feelings are much deeper."

"Nothing says I care for you like plunging a blade in a chest."

Char smiled and nodded before growing serious again.

"And whose fault is that?" she asked, wagging a finger at me. "What made you think using your truesight on her was a wise choice?"

"It wasn't."

"Precisely," she said, slapping her hand down on the marble table. For a brief moment, I thought she would shatter the marble. "You created a bond that cannot be broken while you both live."

"She tried to rectify that the last time we spoke."

"Yet here you sit before me, very much alive," she said with a small smile. "Do you believe for a moment, that if she wants you dead she is incapable of the act?"

"She is quite capable, lethally so."

"Then you understand that you still draw breath because of her feelings for you," she said. "Feelings you only deepened by using your sight. Actions have consequences."

"I didn't know the extent of the consequences at the time."

"And now you do," she answered. "Life is full of lessons— if you live long enough to learn them."

I remained silent for a few seconds.

"Her seeking me out is the worst possible scenario."

"And yet she will," Char said with a faint smile. "These are interlacing threads."

"I don't follow," I said, confused. "Are you saying Regina is somehow connected to Umbra?"

Regina Clark was a darkblade mage who helped me form the Treadwell Supernatural Directive long ago. This was before I became aware of her murderous, sociopathic tendencies.

Her propensity to kill enemies without a second thought, put a considerable damper on our *relationship*. In addition, her being an ancient artifact thief made her a wanted criminal. Every magical authority on the planet wanted her apprehended with extreme prejudice, dead or alive—most of them leaning toward dead.

To say it made things strained between us would be the understatement of the century. Being in her proximity itself was a death sentence; it was not a matter of *if*, but *when*.

I shook my head and refocused on Char.

"Everything is connected—you know this—but I will make it simpler for you," she continued, placing her hand on the surface of the marble table again. Her pale hand was a stark contrast to the black marble. "Look at my hand."

I looked at her hand as it rested on the table.

"Do you see it?" she continued. "Are you looking?"

I nodded.

"Yes, I am looking," I said with a small nod. "I see it."

"Where does my hand end and the table begin?"

"This is making things simpler?"

"Remove your glasses."

I gave her a look of surprise. She never requested I remove my glasses, knowing the depth of my ability, and had instructed me to never use my truesight on her. It's true that I had the ability to see energy signatures, but what made my truesight stand apart was that I could discern the true nature of those I gazed upon.

No one and nothing could hide from my gaze. Intentions, desires, dreams, and weaknesses, all were revealed if I unleashed my truesight. It created a bond that was difficult to break, causing serious repercussions for me and for those I gazed upon.

"Char," I said, dropping the honorific since we were alone. "I don't think that would be such a good idea—for me, that is. You are more than I can process, even when you diminish your signature. Besides, you just gave me a tongue-lashing for using my innersight, now you want me to use it?"

"I didn't say gaze upon me," she snapped. "I said look at my hand, not my soul. I'm not trying to drive you mad. Was I not clear?"

"Perfectly, I just don't think this is such a good idea."

"Thank you, but I don't recall *asking* for your opinion, Sebastian," she said with an edge in her voice. "Remove the glasses and gaze upon my hand."

I removed my glasses and looked at her hand.

A blast of white energy overwhelmed my sense of sight,

blinding me momentarily. When the initial exposure receded somewhat, I was able to focus on her hand. It was vibrant with white energy, while the inert marble of the table was static in contrast.

"What do you see?" she continued. "Tell me."

I knew there was a lesson here for me, but I just wasn't grasping it.

"I'm not seeing what I think you want me to see."

"Stop *thinking* and tell me what you see," she said. "Without emotion or opinion, state what you see."

"Your hand, filled with energy, sitting on the marble which lacks energy," I said. "You expected me to see more?"

"Of course," she said, placing a finger on my forehead, letting a trickle of her power flow into me. "And now?"

Her hand and the marble, though distinct, had somehow managed to merge. The energy from her hand flowed in and around the much slower energy of the marble, which I had failed to notice earlier.

"How?" I asked. "What is that energy coming from the table? What did you do?"

"I merely opened your eyes a little more than usual," she said. "Do you see the connection?"

"Yes."

"Tell me then: where does my hand begin and the table end?"

"There is no end or beginning," I said. "Not one I can see, at least."

"Not yet, no," she replied. "This is an example of you and your Shadow Queen."

"You're saying we're connected, like this?" I asked, pointing at the table. "I don't think we're quite that close."

"No, you're closer."

I shook my head but didn't dare verbally contradict her for various reasons. One, she was a dragon. Two, she had an excellent track record of being correct, as in, practically infallible. Three, she was a dragon. Dragons have been known to rip off arms simply for being irked.

I wasn't about to irk Char.

"Are we talking about the same Regina?" I asked cautiously. "Because the one I know is a heartless, sociopathic murderer. Are you referring to some other Regina I don't know?"

"Being a heartless sociopathic murderer are is considered admirable among my kind," Char said. "She cares deeply for you, enough to risk her life coming to see you."

"I'd prefer she didn't," I said. "Every one of her *visits* usually ends in someone's death."

"I will answer your questions now," she said, completely throwing me off. "First, Fakul Bijan is a mage of considerable power."

"Is he strong enough to siphon another mage inherently?"

"No, he uses an ancient and rare artifact," she said. "The Gauntlet of Mahkah."

She had me at ancient and rare artifact. Something like that would be irresistible to Regina.

"Isn't Mahkah rumored to be the god of vampires?" I asked. "The young woman died devoid of her life-force, not blood."

"Blood is life, but it is not the only source of life," Char said. "This artifact siphons life, not blood, but the end result is the same—it kills the target."

"You think Regina is after this artifact?"

"You know her better than most," Char answered with a nod. "What do *you* think?"

"I think she's going to have a hard time resisting acquiring this artifact," I said. "If it's a gauntlet, where is its mate?"

"Destroyed, long ago. There is only one remaining gauntlet."

"And Fakul is using it," I said. "How did *he* get it?"

"I cannot share that information with you," she said. "Some knowledge needs to remain obscured, for your own safety."

I knew better than to press her on the subject. If she didn't want to share, it was usually in my best interest not to know the answer. It also meant I had asked the right question, but in the wrong manner. I changed topics and shifted my focus.

"What about this organization, Umbra?"

"What of it?"

"Why are they following Fakul?" I asked. "What does he offer them?"

"What do men with little to no power want more than anything else?"

"More power."

She nodded.

"These are dark mages in search of power," she said. "Fakul promises to increase what little they have. It becomes difficult to refuse for those in search of the quick and easy method."

"This gauntlet is both a siphon and augmenter?"

"Yes," Char said. "Any energy siphoned can be imparted to another. Now you know why Fakul has followers."

"Range of use?"

"It requires prolonged contact," she said. "The stronger the target, the longer the contact required. What is your last question, Bas?"

There was never a set number of questions; she would let me ask until she was satisfied she had set me on the right path. She always let me know when I was at my last question.

One more question.

I had an idea of where to find Fakul, or at least his followers. It would be pointless to ask where he was; Char would only inform me that he was in the city. That would be a wasted question. The same logic applied to Regina's where-abouts—Char had already informed me our paths would cross.

I had no doubt that would be the case, especially with a rare, ancient artifact in play. No, I needed something more, something that would give me an advantage against Fakul, or at least told me more about this gauntlet.

I needed to pursue the question she didn't answer, changing it slightly and hoping for the best. This was part of the dance that was asking for information from Char.

Asking the wrong question here would disappoint her and end the conversation, usually with an invitation to leave the Dungeon immediately. If I managed to ask the right question, she could be coaxed into divulging the answer I needed, but not necessarily the answer I wanted.

It was all a game and only she knew the rules.

At her core, I thought Char was just lonely. Very few approached her without fear, with good reason. Approaching a dragon with a large dose of fear was an excellent way to walk away from the interaction intact. But it also meant she had no real friends. I think she rather enjoyed our conversations, though she'd never admit it, and even if I exasperated her at times.

"Where did Fakul get the gauntlet?"

She smiled at me and shook her head.

"You always were a clever child. This, I can answer, but I must warn you," she said, "if you pursue this course, you put the lives of all in your Directive in danger. Do you still want to know?"

"Yes," I said. "If it means preventing more victims of this siphon, they would all ask the same."

"Very well," she said. "Fakul acquired the gauntlet by traveling to the eternal darkness and making a forbidden sacrifice. That is the where, and all I can share with you."

"That sounds more like a how."

"Does it now?" she said, looking away to the side. "When he had completed this act, he was rewarded with the gauntlet, much to the dismay of the authorities present."

When Char said *authorities*, she meant *true authorities*, those who ruled from the shadows, not the Dark or Light Councils. For her, the authorities in our world were faction heads and other dragons, beings with indisputable power —like her.

I nodded.

Her answer wasn't exactly clear, but she tended to wrap her most important answers in riddles. I figured it was a dragon thing, a test to see if I would be willing to decipher her words—again, part of her game.

The 'eternal darkness and a forbidden sacrifice' would require research, but she wasn't going to be clearer than that, and if I asked her, she would tell me she had been more transparent than needed, because she *liked* me.

I never argued with dragon logic, especially when the dragon sitting in front of me could end my life without much effort if angered. Despite enjoying certain privileges extended to me by Char, no one was ever entirely safe around a dragon of any sort, even one that *liked* you.

In most cases, 'liking you' meant looking forward to a quick and painless death, at best, if you angered them, in contrast to a horrific, torturous end if they *didn't* like you. It was always best to err on the side of cautionary preservation of life.

"Thank you, Char," I said with a short bow of my head. "Would you like the payment here, or shall I have it sent to Wei?"

"Here, Bas," she said with a gleam in her eye. "Wei is

currently busy, and I have no desire to disturb him in his duties."

I filed away the information about Tiger. If it was urgent, Char would have told me to get upstairs and deal with Tiger, now. I had a feeling that moment was fast approaching, but I still had time.

I needed to make the most of it.

"As you wish."

I gestured and formed a small, round stone in front of her, about two inches in diameter. It shone bright red in the dim light.

A red diamond.

She nodded approvingly and placed a hand over the gem. A moment later, it was gone.

"This will make a worthy addition to my collection."

What she really meant was *hoard*. She was a dragon after all.

No one knew where Char kept her hoard, and she once told me that she had been growing her collection over millennia. The riches she must have accumulated over that time staggered the imagination.

"Thank you for your answers," I said. "I will deal with Fakul and Umbra."

"Please see that you do," she said, getting slowly to her feet. "These deaths are like ripples. Alone, they seem inconsequential, but if left to continue unchecked, they will bring ruin to this city."

"Understood," I said and pressed my luck, because I occasionally enjoyed living dangerously. "I can't say I'm eager to see Regina again. The last time we spoke, it was a decidedly pointed conversation, with most of the point buried in my chest. It would be helpful to have some idea about when to expect that reunion."

"Are you asking me a question?"

"I wouldn't think of it," I said, feigning innocence. "Especially not after you said I only had one question left. That would be quite rude. You know me, decorum is my middle name."

"I know your middle name, Bas, and decorum is far from it," she said with a small smile, resting a hand on my bent arm as I escorted her out of the conference room. She played the part of ancient elder like a professional, partly because she *was* an ancient elder, and partly because she enjoyed misdirection. "Because I like you, and your payment was acceptable, I will share *some* of what I know."

"No need, Lady Char, you have been more than generous."

"Don't tempt me, and you know I detest obsequiousness," she snapped, squeezing my arm with a grip of steel. "Do you want to know or not?"

"I do," I said, barely able to keep my composure as she dug her fingers into my arm. "Before you snap my arm in half would be ideal."

She laughed and released her grip slightly, letting the blood flow back into my extremity.

"Now *that* is the Bas I know," she said and grew serious. "Your Shadow Queen has been in pursuit of the gauntlet for some time now. She seeks it for another. You must not let her succeed in this, or her other mission."

"Other mission?"

"The gauntlet is the pretense, her true goal is elsewhere. You must stop her from acquiring both."

I knew better than to ask about the true goal.

"She doesn't take rejection well."

Char laughed again, then became silent.

"Be that as it may, I have a request of you," she said, pausing in her steps, causing me to stop walking as a result. "Will you consider the petition of an old dragon?"

This was major.

Char hardly ever made a direct request of me, or anyone for that matter. She viewed it as a form of weakness to require the help of another. It was the typical mindset of dragons, and more so for her. She was fiercely, if not obsessively independent.

"Of course," I said, mildly shocked. "What would you ask?"

"Bring the gauntlet to me," she said, surprising me further. "I will dispose of it properly. Some artifacts should cease to exist, especially one as vile as that. Can you do this?"

"Do I have a choice?"

"Bas, there is *always* a choice," she said. "The issue is not the choice; the issue is living or dying as a consequence of the choice. Which will you choose?"

"I've grown rather fond of living."

"Good choice," she said, patting my arm lightly. "Bring me the gauntlet, and you can continue that trend."

"I will," I said as we walked into the training circle. "Thank you for your time."

I bowed and reflected on how only a dragon could subtly threaten your life and have you thank them for the privilege.

"Think nothing of it," she said, waving my words away, looking up and pausing before refocusing on me. "Go fetch your second, before Wei has to remove her from the premises. That child is stubborn and will be the end of me. She hears nothing I tell her."

I sighed and bowed again.

"As always, it has been a privilege," I said, moving to the stairs as the runes around the circle shifted to lethal. "I will see you soon."

"See that you do."

I left the sub-level and stepped into violence.

EIGHT

A fist crossed past my face nearly colliding with my jaw.

I ducked and slipped to the side, only to see Wei step past me and drive a finger into my would-be attacker's chest. The man flew back, crashing into a wall and sliding slowly to the floor.

"Get her out of here," Wei said, without looking at me. "If she stays, I'm going to have to call Char. I do not want to call Char. *You* do not want me to call Char. You read me?"

"Like a book," I said, scanning the lounge, which had become decidedly hostile in my absence. Several mages gave me death stares, and a few were spooling energy, getting ready to launch attacks. "Where is she?"

"Over there," he motioned with a hooked thumb behind him. "With Bam-bam."

I looked over to where he indicated and noticed that she wasn't exactly *with* Bam-Bam, but more being held in place *by* him. Bam-Bam had her grabbed by the arms and was struggling to keep her away from a group of mages across the floor.

She was being courteous, actually.

I had personally seen her break an ogre's grip on her arm without much effort, and fling said ogre over her shoulder. The fact that Bam-Bam was holding her in place was due to the fact that she was *letting* him hold her in place.

I walked over to where she stood and she smiled at my approach.

I knew this smile.

It was a smile of impending bloodshed.

I needed to get her out of the Dungeon before Char made an appearance. If *that* happened, it was very likely Tiger would be recovering after an extended stay at Haven.

That was something I wanted to avoid.

No one deserved Tiger as a patient.

"Tiger," I said, looking up at Bam-Bam and nodding. "You can let her go. She won't do something rash."

"That would depend on what you consider rash," she said. "Right now I'm considering an advanced eunuch creation program for those mages over there. Would that be rash?"

I glanced over at the group. They were the young and brainless type, more ego than intelligence. If they had gotten on Tiger's bad side—and, in all fairness, Tiger didn't have a good side—they had made a poor choice this evening. One that could get them killed.

Bam-Bam shook his head slowly.

"Wei," I called out, without taking my eyes from the giant in front of me. "Please let Bam-Bam know that Tiger is not suicidal enough to unleash death in the Dungeon, especially when Char specifically informed her not to."

"If she does, this is on you, Sebastian," Wei replied. "BB, let her go."

Bam-Bam looked across at Wei and slowly released Tiger's arms while stepping back. She cracked her neck and rolled her shoulders. Slowly, she turned and looked up into Bam-Bam's face.

"Thank you, big guy," she said, patting him on the arm and rolling a shoulder again. "I think you helped me work out a kink that's been nagging me for weeks."

Bam-Bam looked down and nodded.

Tiger stepped away and walked over to where Wei stood. Wei tensed as she stepped close.

"Don't," Wei said. "Just don't. They're not worth it."

"Relax," Tiger said as she walked past him. "I'm just going to have a word."

"That's what concerns me," he said. "Your words have a way of killing people."

Tiger walked over to the group of mages.

I counted at least five of them, with the leader obviously standing in front of the group and putting on a brave face as Tiger closed on them. If he was smart, he would keep his mouth shut and say nothing.

If he felt he needed to demonstrate his position in the pack and exert his dominance over this woman with an attitude, he was going to be in for a rude awakening. Tiger wasn't an imposing presence, at least not until the bleeding started. Then, she could be downright heart-stopping in her ability to unleash death and devastation.

I moved quickly and arrived at Tiger's side before she could say anything.

"I'm sure this has all been some kind of misunderstanding," I said, stepping in front of Tiger. "I truly apologize. What's your name?"

Smug bravado covered the mage's expression.

He was young *and* foolish.

Too young to realize when he was inches away from a sudden, painful death.

"Emerson," said the young mage. "This your woman?"

"For all intents and purposes, yes," I lied. "How about all

of your drinks are complimentary for the rest of the evening? On me?"

"All night for me *and* my group?"

"Of course," I said. "For you and your group. Wei?"

"Done," Wei said. "All your drinks are courtesy of Mr. Treadwell tonight."

"Excellent," Emerson said, turning to his group of sycophants. "See, boys? That's how you handle the situation. You put the smartass bitch in her place, and her simpy boyfriend pays for your drinks. Weakness always recognizes strength."

They all had a good laugh at my expense. I stepped to the side as Tiger stepped forward.

Emerson turned to face her. I almost pitied him.

"What did you say?" Tiger asked in a low voice. "Say that again?"

Emerson, who clearly lacked any sense of self-preservation, took a step forward. Out of the corner of my eye, I saw Wei shake his head as he headed back to the bar in the center of the floor.

"I said, weakness always recognizes strength," Emerson repeated. "Are you hard of hearing too? What are you going to do about it? Tell your *weak* boyfriend to fix me? He's already buying me and my crew drinks. What's he going to do next? Dinner and a massage?"

"He's all yours," I said, stepping further away. "It seems a lesson is in order."

Emerson looked at me and laughed.

"A lesson?" he mocked. "By who? You?"

"Don't kill him," I said as I walked past Tiger and headed over to join Wei. "Char would *not* be pleased."

Tiger nodded without taking her eyes off Emerson.

"Refresh my memory," Tiger said, looking up as she stepped close to Emerson, who towered over her. "Can you repeat what you said?"

Emerson turned to his group and laughed.

"I called your boyfriend a weak simp."

"No, I heard that part," Tiger said with a smile. If Emerson had any common sense, that smile would have set off every internal alarm he possessed, driving him out of the Dungeon at a dead run. Sadly, common sense was anything but common these days. "What did you say *before* that?"

By this point, all of Emerson's friends had stepped back. Some part of their limbic brains had realized they were standing in the presence of a predator, and they were the bloody and weak prey. Emerson looked around, noticed he was standing alone, and made the unwise choice of trying to save face.

I felt sorry for him, but he had made several tactical errors.

The first was engaging Tiger in the first place. She was an unassuming woman, but she radiated heart-stopping pain when angry. And she had started her evening in a simmering rage. The second error he committed and probably the most egregious, was that he doubled down on insulting her.

Tiger didn't take insults well. It stemmed from her childhood, and was a sore subject for her, and especially anyone who directed insults at her.

The smugness returned to Emerson's face.

He looked down and sneered at her.

"I called your boyfriend a simp and you a smartass bi—"

He never managed to finish the sentence.

Not for lack of desire. I'm certain he *wanted* to finish that sentence, it was just that the right cross Tiger unleashed on his face disconnected his brain from his speech center, along with his jaw, prohibiting all forms of speech.

For Emerson, it was probably a matter of things happening too fast for him to realize. Tiger possessed preternatural speed, which she utilized with deadly efficiency in combat.

Before he could react, Tiger had unleashed a fist to his jaw, causing Emerson to become airborne. He crashed into a far wall, unconscious before he hit the floor. His group of friends rushed over to where he lay, but none dared to move against Tiger.

It appeared there was *some* intelligence in the group after all.

She had held back though—since his jaw was still connected to the rest of his face. That was nice of her, considering her usual response involved someone leaving existence as they knew it.

Wei stared at her as she approached.

"What?" she said. "I didn't kill him. He may not be able to speak for a few months, but he's alive. I'd call that a win."

"You are insane," Wei said, staring at her. "That strike could have killed him."

"But it didn't, check for yourself," she said. "He's still breathing—it'll be mostly through his nose—but he's breathing. I broke his jaw, but I left his spine intact. That's called mercy where I come from."

"Out. Now," Wei said, pointing to the exit. "Don't make me repeat myself. Sebastian, *you* are always welcome back, alone. You"—he stared hard at Tiger—"don't visit for a few months."

"Fine," Tiger said, heading for the exit. "I'll meet you outside, Sebastian."

"She's just on edge," I said by way of apology. "We're working a case and it's hitting a little too close to home."

"That's why she's walking out of here and not being carried out," Wei said. "You need to get her under control, Sebastian. Her *hit first, ask later* policy in life is going to get her killed one day, and you along with her."

"I'll take that into consideration."

"See that you do," Wei said as he headed over to the still-unconscious Emerson. "Be safe."

"I'll do my best," I said as I headed out. "Thanks."

"Don't mention it, ever."

I headed out of the Dungeon.

NINE

Tiger stood outside with Fuxi and Numa.

The Twins seemed to be at ease and rightfully so. If there existed anyone outside of Char or myself who could handle Tiger, it was these two.

"...so then I ripped the ogre's arm off and beat him with it," Tiger said as I walked into the conversation. "After that, I let Ox have him."

Nuwa smiled at Tiger's story, and Fuxi while he listened, maintained his vigilance on the entrance. Trying to get past the Twins of Death without authorization was one of the fastest ways to get admitted to Haven's emergency room.

"Your vehicle will be arriving shortly, Mr. Treadwell," Fuxi said. "I took the liberty of having it brought up after Ms. Tiger informed us of the evening's events."

"You mean the events where she broke a mage's jaw?"

"He deserved that," Tiger said. "He insulted me—which would have been reason enough—but he had started by calling us a bunch of hacks who served no purpose in the city."

"Which you know to be false," I said calmly. "We have a

clear and distinct purpose as the bulwarks against criminality run amok."

"I know and I tried to explain it to him, not exactly in those words, but you know, the general idea of—we help those who have nowhere to turn," she said. "He called me a liar and a grifter."

"Grifter?" I said, slightly surprised. "That's a new one."

"Now, you know me, I have thick skin," she said with a straight face. "I can take an insult most of the time."

I raised an eyebrow.

"Like the one he unleashed on you, not five minutes ago?" I asked. "Nearly punching his head off his shoulders was an excellent demonstration of restraint."

"Let me finish," Tiger said, raising a finger. "You came in at the tail end of that conversation. I had—"

"I seem to recall requiring you to exit the Dungeon a few months ago because someone called you, and I quote, 'a mad dog knocker that should be put out of her misery for the safety of mankind' unquote," Nuwa said. "You put that mage in Haven for several months with an assortment of breaks."

"Not an assortment," Fuxi added. "If I recall, she broke every bone in both of his arms, then informed him that the correct term is kinetic mage, not knocker."

"He called me a mad dog," she protested, "and a knocker and a danger to mankind."

"Good thing you can take an insult most of the time," I said. "What did the young clueless mage say this evening that set you off? Aside from calling you a grifter?"

"He called us, the Directive, worthless," she said, her voice low and dangerous. "That we let people die because we're worthless."

Fuxi and Nuwa stepped back and remained silent.

Everyone knew that insulting Tiger was taking a chance at visiting Haven for an extended stay. The only thing worse than that was insulting the Directive. That was taking a chance at an early grave.

For Tiger, the Directive was her family. You insulted or threatened them at your peril, which was considerable when it came to angering Tiger.

"That was unwise," Nuwa said. "Will we be notifying next of kin?"

"I left him alive," Tiger said with a sigh. "He won't be speaking for a bit—having your mouth wired shut makes conversation tough."

"You left him alive?" Fuxi asked, surprised. "I must commend your restraint, Ms. Tiger. That is exceptional."

"I know, right?" Tiger said, glancing at me with a smile of triumph. "Go, me."

"Please don't encourage her," I said as my vehicle arrived. "She should have entirely refrained from rearranging his face." I turned to the Twins and bowed. "May you both have an uneventful evening."

"It has always been the case after Ms. Tiger leaves the premises, that the evenings remain calm," Nuwa said. "For that, we are grateful. Please have a safe journey home."

They both returned my bow.

"See?" Tiger said as we headed to the Tank. "I'm a calming influence on the Dungeon. They're actually thankful to have me there."

"Thankful to have you leave is probably more accurate," I said. "Get in and I'll bring you up to speed on my conversation with Char."

We headed over to the Tank.

I placed a hand on its body, and the doors unlocked as a subtle orange wave of energy raced across the chassis.

My vehicle was a SuNaTran masterpiece, merging automotive and runic design into a virtually indestructible method of transport. Cecil had taken the body of a 1966 Lincoln Continental and had transformed it into what I lovingly dubbed the Tank.

He had generously offered me something called the Montague Package, which I declined, informing him that there had better be a comparable Treadwell package.

He assured me that he would create one just for the Tank.

It was that set of runes which graced my indestructible vehicle currently. The Tank had been extensively runed and modified to withstand virtually every type of magical and conventional attack. It was even Tiger-proof. The matte black exterior melted into the night as we got in and pulled away from the Dungeon.

I shared the information about Fakul Bijan and Umbra first. She took that information relatively well, expressing a desire to dismember the members of Umbra, tonight if possible. There was a reason I waited until we were in the Tank before bringing up Regina.

I shared that information after discussing Umbra.

Tiger drove a fist into the glove compartment when I shared what Char told me about Regina seeking me out. The damage was almost instantly repaired once she removed her hand. Cecil was truly a master of his craft.

"Has Char lost her fucking mind?"

"Would you like me to go back?" I asked. "You could go ask her, though I would express the sentiment differently, if I were you."

"Not even remotely funny," she said, shooting me a dark look. "Regina is toxic to everyone, especially *you*."

"I have no idea what you mean."

"Don't you dare give me the innocent play," she snapped. "That bond you share seems to short-circuit your brain."

"What are you implying? That I lose the ability to think for myself due to a truesight bond?"

"That's *exactly* what I'm saying," she said, raising her voice. "There's no implication, it's fact."

"I think you're exaggerating," I replied, keeping my eyes on the road to avoid crushing any of the vehicles whose drivers jeopardized their lives by cutting in front of me. "There is no known, documented instance of a truesight bond negatively affecting cognition. Do you have proof of this effect?"

"I don't need proof," Tiger replied with a low growl. "I see it with my own eyes. Your brain becomes all mushy, and you stop thinking straight around her. Then she bats her eyelashes and uses those puppy dog eyes, and you're done. Next thing we know, we're on a heist, stealing some ancient jewel of power with half the Councils after us. Did you forget what happened last time?"

"I have not," I said. "That was simply a series of misunderstandings."

"Misunderstandings? You must be delusional, " she shot back. "Regina had stolen a jewel of negation and conveniently failed to mention it until that sect of furious negomancers showed up looking for blood. Our blood. Tell me again, how was that a misunderstanding?"

"They made the mistake of trusting Regina around an artifact of that power," I said. "Once she appropriated it—"

"Stole it," Tiger interrupted. "Don't make it pretty. She's a cutthroat thief, plain and simple."

"In any case," I continued, "she misunderstood how determined they would be to get their jewel back, and they misunderstood how lethal she could be."

"People died, lots of people died, because of her."

"I'm aware," I said. "Not to mention the hit the Directive took to repair our somewhat shady reputation with the negomancers since she—"

"She said she was acting as a member of the Directive and

needed to ascertain the security of the gem," Tiger finished. "She used us, then dragged our name through the mud to get what she wanted. She's an evil, heartless bitch. We need to stay away from her, and when I say *we,* I mean *you.*"

"I don't think we can avoid it," I said, accelerating the Tank. "Char wants the gauntlet, and so does Regina. Which of those two do you think it will be easier to convince?"

"Well, slash me sideways and split me open," she said in her usual colorful way. "This is going to suck no matter which way it goes, isn't it?"

"I'm afraid I have to agree."

"Fine, let's get to the Church," she said. "I need to prepare if Regina is coming back into our lives."

TEN

"No attempted murdering," I said as I parked the Tank. "From you or the others. I mean it this time."

"Last time was self-defense."

"I don't see how trying to exterminate her with a solid blast of air qualifies as self-defense."

"I was being proactive," Tiger said. "With your woman, it's kill or be killed."

"She is not my woman."

"I don't think your brain got that memo—try sending it again," she said. "Hopefully it will stick this time."

"No being proactive this time," I said. "Perhaps if you don't try to kill her, she will refrain from trying to drive a blade into your chest."

"If I remember, the only one with a blade in his chest was a certain lovestruck mage who, for all his ability to see, missed the obvious danger right in front of his face."

"She is not a danger."

"She does have a way of making a point, though. Did you even feel the blade go in when she betrayed you and the Directive? Or were you still thinking she wasn't a danger?"

"What she and I have is...complicated," I said.

"Your level of delusion must be amazing to experience," she said, shaking her head. "Wait until I tell the others—they will be absolutely thrilled to hear she's paying us a visit."

"Just try not to kill her," I said with a sigh, placing a hand on the dash and turning the engine off. "At least for the first five minutes. Think you can manage that?"

"I won't attempt to rip her head off if she behaves," Tiger said as we stepped out of the Tank. "She tries anything suicidal, like using those stupid blades of hers, and all bets are off."

"Fair enough."

There was no way I would convince her to leave Regina alone. They were too much alike and there was too much bad blood between them. The most I could expect was a hostile detente until the first blow was attempted.

Then all hell would break loose.

Five minutes was being optimistic.

We crossed the underground garage that sat under the Church, our new headquarters situated under the Basilica of St. Patrick's Old Cathedral, on 263 Mulberry Street, in the heart of Nolita—North of Little Italy.

The Directive had relocated into certain parts of the catacombs—the only remaining catacombs in the city, to my knowledge—for security purposes. We updated the defenses, leaving the main historical areas untouched, and added to the tunnels where needed or required.

In essence, we had created a separate set of catacombs to act as our headquarters. Tiger had immediately wanted to dub the new headquarters, the Cave.

I quickly shut that idea down, knowing it was only a matter of time before the Cave devolved into something associated with bats.

We needed to maintain standards, after all.

Our previous headquarters, The White House, located at

262 Central Park West, had undergone extensive renovations with the goal of killing the members of the Directive, courtesy of Verity, a self-appointed, semi-deluded organization of mages intent on policing and controlling the magical population around the planet.

It appeared that Verity held a grudge about my involvement in assisting my cousin, Tristan, and his associate, Strong, in handing them their asses. They sent me an explosive message and I took that opportunity to relocate the Directive.

What Verity lacked in intelligence, they made up for in numbers and guile. I was fairly certain more reprisals would be arriving in the future, but unlike my cousin, they would find that I played by a different set of rules.

Although I wasn't keen on vengeance—finding it a useless waste of time and resources—to target my family or the Directive incurred my wrath. Threaten me and I would retaliate in kind. After all, all was fair in love and war. I never took personal attacks, personally.

Threaten my family, however, and I would raze the earth to exact the measure of vengeance I felt was adequate. Verity would soon find this out, but first, we had more pressing matters to deal with, starting with Umbra and Fakul.

Tiger and I headed across the garage to the reinforced door that led to the headquarters. This door had been specially designed to stop practically anything and everything from breaching the interior of the headquarters; it was made of Australian Buloke and reinforced with rune-infused titanium.

In order to properly test its defensive properties, I had let Tiger and the rest of the Directive try their best to destroy it prior to installation. The best that they could do collectively was scratch the surface.

Satisfied with the strength of the door, I had set about

reinforcing the walls, floor, and ceiling around the door to the same degree of effectiveness, and again, let them have a go at breaching the headquarters.

To date, no one in the Directive had found a method of getting past the entrance. To incentivize the plan, I offered whoever could break past the defenses a new custom-runed weapon of their choice, forged in the same manner as the door.

So far, no one had managed to claim the prize.

"Who was the last to attempt the door prize?" I asked as we approached the massive entrance. "Do you know?"

She nodded.

"Ox thought he had it figured out," she said with a smile. "Nearly broke his hand in the process of trying."

"What did he use?"

"Tempered phasic mace he found in the armory," she said as I placed a hand on the door, setting the runes inscribed on its surface ablaze in various shades of orange and red. "Turns out it wasn't as strong as he thought. Shattered it on the second swing, sprained his wrist, and nearly put an eye out."

"A phasic weapon would be ineffective on the runes inscribed on the door," I said. "Didn't you tell him?"

"I wanted to see what would happen," she said with a mischievous smile. "I did tell him to pick another weapon, though."

"I worry about you sometimes."

"So do I," she answered with a small laugh. "Sometimes, I scare myself."

"Have you given it a go?"

She shook her head.

"I already tried to destroy this thing," she said, pointing at the massive door as it swung open silently. "All I managed to do was scratch it." She rubbed a hand over the small, but deep gouge that remained in the surface. "If that's all I can do, I doubt they're going to have better luck."

"Doesn't hurt to try," I said as we stepped inside. "Assemble everyone on site in the conference room. Who's currently in the field?"

"According to the operations schedule, half the Directive is out on missions," she said as we walked the catacombs. "Rat, Ox, Rabbit, Snake, and Goat are in house. Everyone else is abroad."

"I see," I said, tapping my chin. "Have everyone except Goat gather in the conference room. I'll meet with them shortly."

"Where are you going?"

"I need to ask Goat some questions about this gauntlet we're supposed to locate," I said. "Maybe he has some insight into its properties that Char was reluctant to share."

"That's Char with everything," she said. "She never speaks clearly."

"It's what makes her Char," I said. "Make sure Rat has any details he found on the Jane Doe ready for review. I'd like to know if she had any next of kin in the city; they deserve to know what happened to her."

Tiger nodded and headed down a corridor.

"See you in ten?" she asked.

"More like fifteen," I said. "I'll be brief with Goat, but you know how he gets if I don't stop him."

"He needs to get out more, maybe make some friends," she said, walking away. "Going outside and touching grass is good for you."

"Last time he tried that, it didn't exactly turn out well."

Tiger laughed as she kept walking.

"And you call *me* the dangerous one."

Each member of the Directive had their own idiosyncrasies. In Goat's case, he was acutely agoraphobic, harboring a severe dislike for open or public spaces and crowds of people. He preferred staying in the armory, forging weapons for the Directive.

It was the one place where he felt at ease and I left him to it. In his armory, he crafted rune-inscribed weapons like my twin karambits, and rarely felt the need to leave the comfort of his forge.

I made it a point never to force him into the field unless it was absolutely necessary, and even then he would travel in the Hammer, a portable forge which was housed in one of the Directive's large assault vehicles.

I walked the catacombs, careful to make the proper turns at the appropriate intersections. The catacombs looked simple, but were actually designed to be Corridors of Chaos, courtesy of Sister Heka from the Wordweavers.

She and Goat were close friends and shared techniques as well as knowledge about the runes used on weapons. If Goat proved to be a dead end, I would have to pay her a visit to find out more about this gauntlet.

I didn't exactly relish the idea of paying Aria and her Wordweavers a visit. She and I held vastly different opinions on the proper use of power. For me, magical power and energy manipulation was a means to an end. For her and the Wordweavers the power was the end to be used only to help others.

I partly agreed with her.

It was where we disagreed that had proven to be an insurmountable wall between us. In the end, we agreed to disagree, rather than jeopardize our deep friendship.

She still frowned on the activities of the Directive, but she never involved herself in our affairs, if she could help it. From my end, I made it a point to never involve the Wordweavers in Directive affairs, and as such we maintained a delicate balance.

I turned down several more corridors, still lost in thought, when I heard the sound of metal on metal, which meant Goat was busy. He preferred not to be disturbed when working on a project, but this couldn't wait.

I pushed the large, steel door open, braced myself against the wall of heat that wrapped itself around me, and peered into the forge.

The heat of the forge was nearly unbearable, but it never seemed to bother Goat. Several furnaces were bright with flames, and I could see various projects in different states of completion.

Goat stood in the center of the floor over a large anvil, hammer in hand as he pounded on a red-hot piece of metal. In stature, he was almost as large as Ox, but where Ox was outgoing and social, Goat was withdrawn and reserved.

"Hello, Goat," I called out, the sound of the hammer impacting the metal drowning out my voice. "Goat!"

He struck the metal a few more times before looking up to acknowledge my presence. He gave me a short nod and motioned for me to close the door.

I did as he suggested, while he put the metal back in one of the furnaces. He gave it a glance, waved a hand at the steel and then focused on me. I knew he preferred working on his metal more than engaging in conversation with me, unless we discussed weaponry.

His ability to manipulate metals—ferromancy—made him the ideal weapon-smith. He possessed the ability to affect metal on a molecular level, transforming it as he wished.

"Director," he said in his low, gravelly voice. "I'm a little busy. How can I help you?"

"How are you, Goat?" I said, looking around the windowless space. The forge was large, easily forty feet across and twice as wide. "How are you enjoying the new space?"

"It's functional and practical," he said—which by Goat's standards was a ringing endorsement. "It suits me fine."

"I'm glad to hear it," I said. "I have a question for you."

His eyes lit up. He knew that when I came to him with questions, it would be for a weapon research project that would usually produce said weapon.

"Ask," he said. "If I know, so will you."

"The Gauntlet of Mahkah," I said. "Have you ever heard of this weapon?"

He rubbed his chin with the back of a gloved hand as he gave it some thought. He put down his hammer which was at least twice the size of any regular smithing hammer, and removed his gloves.

"It's not a weapon," he said, moving from the anvil across the floor to an extensive library of oversized books. He searched the shelves for a few seconds, before settling on one, pulling one of the large tomes from a shelf. "Well, not *just* a weapon."

He brought the book over to a large, metal worktable and opened it, pointing to the page. I approached, giving the furnace a wide berth to avoid being scorched.

I looked at the image.

"Is that it?" I asked. "What is it made of?"

"Nightmares and death," he said. "This is a cursed item."

ELEVEN

"A cursed item?" I asked. "Meaning what, exactly?"

"Nothing good."

This was a typical conversation with Goat.

He occasionally preferred to speak indirectly with metaphors, similes, and philosophical descriptors, unless the subject was the fabrication of a particular weapon. We hadn't gotten to that part yet, so I had to traverse the ethereal before we could discuss the concrete.

"What causes it to be cursed?"

He looked at the page closely.

"See these runes here?" he said, pointing to a section of the gauntlet. "These runes make it a force siphon. That's bad news if you're on the wrong end of this thing."

"Do you know what it's made of?" I asked, looking at the image of the black metal gauntlet. Even in the image, it gave off a feeling of evil, which immediately set me on edge. How could a gauntlet be evil? "What kind of metal is that? Steel?"

He shook his head.

"This metal is harder. Tungsten," he said knowingly. "Impossible to work with, without knowing how."

"Can anyone make a set of these, or do they need to have your ability?"

"My ability and more," he said. "My ability to work the metal, but more to inscribe the runes. These weren't created by one person."

"How many would be needed to create them?" I asked. "Two? Three?"

"At least three," he said, still looking at the image. "Two with my ability to shape and hold the metal, and one powerful mage to inscribe and shape the runes. A very powerful mage with runes."

"How long would it take?"

"Three days after getting the base metal."

"Three days?" I asked surprised, expecting weeks or months. "That's it?"

"Three *unbroken* days holding the casts in place," he said. "Seventy-two hours of non-stop casting for three people, while using energy, and working the hardest metal, as it resists every shaping. Even I can't do that."

"Three unbroken days," I repeated. "That certainly changes things. That sounds dangerous."

He nodded.

"Fatal, if not strong enough," he said. "Unbroken casting for 24 hours is very hard. Two days? Only masters try that. Three days? No one tries that."

"Is it that hard?"

"The mages who try usually end up broken or worse," he said, still gazing at the image in the book. "Even with a dual cast...too dangerous."

"Dual cast?"

"One mage starts, holds the cast for a few hours, second mage steps in and takes over," he said by way of explanation. "Only way I would do it, and it's still dangerous. Need someone as good or better than me—not easy."

"Indeed," I said, giving it some thought. Goat was considered a rare ferromancer—even by other ferromancers—able to manipulate metals in ways never before seen. "Could you create this now?"

"Too difficult to create now," he said. "Those runes are too hard to copy, and you need a powerful rune mage to inscribe the metal."

"Not to mention, two ferromancers," I said. "Finding one is hard enough, but two with your ability? That is quite difficult."

"Like I said, too difficult to create now."

"What exactly do you mean by a powerful rune mage?" I asked, looking at the notes on the gauntlet. They were written in a language I couldn't decipher. I had an idea what he meant, but I wanted to make sure. "Can you be a bit more specific?"

"Not a regular mage," he said as if that made it clearer. "A mage that can shape runes the way I shape metal. A rune mage."

"You mean a Wordweaver?"

He gave it some thought and then nodded.

"Wordweaver can be two, rune mage and metal shaper," he said. "Can make it a dual cast."

It certainly fit the description. Wordweavers shaped reality with the power of their words and runes, the same way other mages used energy and symbols. Getting a Wordweaver willing to do this would be near impossible.

"Would you be able to replicate it," I continued, "if I brought you one of these gauntlets?"

He remained silent, thinking.

"I can copy the runes and examine the craftsmanship," he said. "I don't think I could make one."

"Understood," I said, looking away to the furnaces. Time

to switch tacks. "How would you go about destroying one of these?"

He opened his eyes a little wider as he stared at me.

"I wouldn't," he said. "These are special. Dangerous but special."

"You wouldn't or couldn't?"

"Both," he said. "Wouldn't because too rare. Couldn't because trying would kill me."

"What if you had no choice?" I pressed. We had often engaged in these kinds of thought exercises when facing or creating specialized weapons. Creating weapons, without discussing their weaknesses or methods of destruction, made no sense. You never knew when that information could save your life. "How would *you* destroy it?"

He rubbed his chin with the back of his hand again.

"In steps," he said. "All at once would create an explosion. A big explosion." He spread his arms out as far as he could to emphasize how large. "First, you have to destroy the runes, or it will siphon the energy of anything you use against it."

"If I manage to destroy the runes, doesn't it just become a very strong gauntlet?"

He shook his head.

"For the creation process to work, these have to be made with rune-infused tungsten," he said. "The outside runes just allow the siphon and sharing. They are still powerful as a weapon."

"So they're indestructible?"

"Didn't say that—just really hard to destroy," he said. "I couldn't do it, you couldn't do it. Needs heat, hotter than any furnace I have, to damage the runes. To completely destroy the gauntlet, you need a void."

"A what?"

"A...void," he said slowly as if I didn't understand the

words he was using. "A space of emptiness and darkness. No light, only pressure. Like a small black hole."

"I see," I said. "Can I assume you don't possess the means to create a void?"

"No," he said, shaking his head. "Need an advanced negomancer to make one of those; even then, it's still too dangerous."

"Why?"

"Gauntlet has energy. Energy can't be destroyed. Only—"

"Transformed," I finished. "By compressing it in this void, we need to direct the energy that's being released."

He nodded.

"Energy in the gauntlet has to go somewhere if you destroy it," he said. "Negomancer has to create a void, and then *hold* it closed. Like trying to hold an explosion in your hands. One mistake and...boom. No more negomancer."

"The negomancer needs to contain the explosion?"

He nodded again.

"Needs to hold the void closed," he said. "Need a very strong negomancer for that."

"I don't know any strong negomancers. Actually, I don't know any negomancers." Which wasn't entirely true. Regina had some negomantic ability. I brushed the thought away. "Do you?"

He shook his head.

"More rare than ferromancers," he said, pointing to the image of the gauntlet. "Are you getting one of them?"

"There's only one left," I said, looking at the image again. "Char wants me to give it to her, if I do get it."

He shook his head slowly.

"Too dangerous, even for Char."

"I was thinking the same thing," I said. "If I do manage to acquire it, can you create a copy from the original?"

"Need runed tungsten. I can create a good fake, but not exact."

"How good of a fake?" I asked as a plan began formulating in my mind. "Would it be good enough to fool Char?"

He narrowed his eyes at me.

"This is a dangerous game, Director," he said with a smile. I knew I had sold him on the challenge. "Are you keeping it?"

"I'm not, *you* are," I said, pointing at him. "If you can make a copy authentic enough to fool Char, it will buy us time. Then you can keep the original and find a way to reverse engineer it. Think you can do it?"

He nodded.

"Would need help. Heka," he said thoughtfully. "We should still destroy it...it's dangerous. Too much power in one item."

"I have every intention of destroying it," I said. "I want you to be able to replicate its siphoning properties. Are you sure you need Heka?"

"Yes, she is good. Better than me."

High praise coming from Goat.

"I'm not a fan of involving the Wordweavers."

He shrugged his shoulders.

"Heka is the best."

He was basically telling me it was either Heka or no one. I disliked having limited options. There were also other concerns.

I wasn't fond of the idea of bringing Heka in on this for several reasons. If Char found out, her retribution would be absolutely biblical; I preferred to leave the Wordweavers out of her crosshairs.

There was also the matter of what the gauntlet could do. Siphoning and imparting power meant there would be several parties interested in acquiring the gauntlet for their own selfish agendas.

I wasn't keen on pointing those interested parties in Aria's direction. Then there was the possibility of Aria wanting to retain possession of the gauntlet for the safety of everyone involved.

I preferred to keep it as a deterrent.

Even Char, who professed to want to destroy it for the good of others, was lying. At best, she would hoard it. At worst, she would bestow it upon another, or use it as a bargaining chip in one of her plays for power.

In addition, Regina was trying to get it for some unknown buyer.

The best result would be for the gauntlet to disappear.

The next best result would be to convince everyone it was destroyed, while disappearing it ourselves. Involving Heka was risky, but it now seemed it was a risk we would have to take.

"Are you sure you need Heka?"

"Plus one more: Aria," he said, completely blindsiding me. "She is strong enough for the runes."

"You want me to get Aria involved?" I said. "She would never go for my plan. You and Heka will have to recreate the runes."

"Won't be perfect," he warned. "She is one of the best."

"It's a risk we will have to take," I said. "Getting Aria involved in inscribing runes is a non-starter."

"Or you could just give the gauntlet to Char."

"You know we can't do that," I said. "It's too dangerous."

"Dangerous to give and dangerous to keep," he said with a smile. "Pick your dangerous."

"I don't know why I thought this would be straightforward," I grumbled. "Let me speak to the others; I'll let you know within the hour."

He nodded, put his gloves on again, and picked up his massive hammer as he walked over to one of the furnaces.

"I'll get ready."

I walked out of the oppressive heat of the forge.

He and I both knew which dangerous I would pick.

TWELVE

I arrived at the conference room with thoughts of death on my mind.

Rat, Ox, and Tiger were sitting around the circular conference table. The table was large enough for the twelve members of the Directive to sit comfortably around it, though we rarely had the full Directive in the headquarters at any one time unless it was a matter of survival.

The yellow-orange wood of the table had hints of deep reds, and had been a gift from an associate of Char, another dragon who collected rare furniture and felt this table was perfect for us.

Unlike the door to the headquarters, it was made of rune-inscribed Persian ironwood, and shaped into an impressive piece of ancient Persian craftsmanship that dated back several thousand years. It was considered priceless.

"I have a proposal," I said, taking my seat. I looked around and paused. "Where are Snake and Rabbit?"

"Snake is in her lab, she will be up in ten," Tiger said. "Rabbit is relaying information to Dog, who is in deep-cover."

"What information?" I asked. "Do I have a brief on this?"

"On your desk," Rat said. "It has to do with that Jane Doe. Turns out she was a Light Council mage working a case."

"Bloody hell," I said, running a hand through my hair. "That complicates things. What case was she working?"

"Mage deaths of the unusual sort," Rat said, "most of them happening in no-man's land, uptown."

"Unusual sort? Like?"

"Siphoned of all life-force," he said. "Once Dog gets the information, he can point us in the right direction."

"She got too close, and someone decided to close her case," Tiger said. "You want me to call Honor?"

"No, I better pay him a visit," I said, not looking forward to that particular conversation. "I'm going to assume Tiger brought you all up to speed on the Regina situation?"

Rat and Ox looked at each before looking at me and nodded.

"Good, let me share my thoughts on our next steps."

I told them the plan I had discussed with Goat about creating an alternate gauntlet and keeping the original for reverse engineering.

I sat back and observed them once I was finished.

I had known each of them long enough to know how they were thinking. Add that to the fact that my ability allowed me to read them and their intentions. It wasn't as accurate as telepathy, but it let me know their general thoughts.

Tiger was excited—probably at the prospect of confronting Char on something as dangerous as withholding an item of this importance. She was fearless and enjoyed facing death on a regular basis.

Rat was pensive and most likely considering how to pull this off while incurring minimal losses on our end. He would propose a plan that would be risky, but require minimal personnel.

Ox would be the first to speak. He would advise against it, and his first 'gut feeling' would be to walk away from this. Keeping everyone alive would be next to impossible even without Char getting involved. If she did get directly involved, he would inform me that going to war would be a losing proposition.

"This is a bad idea, Boss," Ox said. "We don't want to go to war with Char or her people. It would be a massacre."

"For them," Tiger said with a smile. "If Goat can make a reasonable copy, we can pull this off."

"Why?" Rat asked in his quiet voice. "Why do you want this gauntlet?"

"I don't," I said. "I want the ability it possesses. Being able to siphon or impart energy is an excellent deterrent, and we have no shortage of enemies."

"If those enemies find out we have something like that, they're going to get real curious," Ox said. "Homicidally curious."

"How long can you keep this information in-house?"

"If it's just us? Pretty much indefinitely," Ox said. "If Regina finds out or Char figures out the switch, a few days. Regina will leak it to make a play for it, and Char will do it to teach us a lesson. I'm more concerned about Char, obviously. Are you sure you want to butt heads with her?"

"It's not just me," I said, placing both hands on the table. "If I do this, it directly affects the Directive; all our lives will be in danger. I won't make this op mandatory. If you feel it's too risky, this is your chance to walk away."

They all stared at me.

Being part of the Treadwell Supernatural Directive was entirely voluntary. It was true that many of the members owed me their lives, but I'd made it clear from the onset that life-debts did not factor in to being a part of the Directive.

"Our lives were in danger the moment we joined the Directive. I'm in," Tiger said as I knew she would. "This is going to be interesting."

"You know I'm in, Boss," Ox said. "I'll work out how to increase personal security around here and individually. I'll also look for chinks in Char's security setup, just in case. I'm not looking forward to dancing with Fuxi and Numa, but I'd rather do it prepared than surprised."

I nodded and looked at Rat.

He steepled his hands and stared back, his face impassive.

"I have a few devices I need to field test," Rat said, brushing some hair from his face. "This op would be an ideal stress test. Do we know where this Fakul Bijan is currently headquartered?"

"No, but I'll leave that to you," I said. "Tiger, I need you to inform the rest of the available Directive. Same option applies. Let me know if anyone wants to sit this one out."

"You know they won't," she said. "I don't know why you even bother asking."

"Because it's the right thing to do," I said. "I do not carelessly throw lives away. Facing Char is suicide in most cases. Pissing her off before facing her is certain death."

"But you have a plan, don't you?" Tiger said. "I mean, besides the fake gauntlet Goat is creating, you have something else, something deeper."

"I do," I said. "It's risky and most likely will get me killed if I fail, but a plan is in place."

"Good," she said with a smile that invited death. "I get first crack at Fakul."

"We need to find him first," I said, standing. "Rat, once you do, relay the message to Tiger. Once we have that information, we'll plan a visit to Umbra and Fakul. No one goes dark until then. I should be back by the time Rat locates Umbra."

"Where are you going?" Tiger asked.

"I'm going to inform Honor about his mage, and see if I can find out more about the case that Jane Doe was working on."

"He's not going to be happy. Do you need company?"

"No," I said. "Give Rahbi a call to let Honor know I'm paying him a visit, then start working out the logistics of a small-scale assault on a fortified position. I'm sure Umbra will have superior numbers and some hardened location. Run the simulations and make sure we have a chance of walking out alive."

Tiger nodded.

"What about Char?"

"There are no simulations that can help us with her," I said. "Run strategies using the Dungeon as a staging area, factoring in Wei's security team along with Fuxi and Numa."

"Those two are going to be a problem."

"Not if we neutralize them first."

"You think we can neutralize the Twins of Death?" she asked. "Did Goat hit you with a hammer while you were paying him a visit?"

"Together it would be nearly impossible; we would need to divide and conquer with them."

"Do you want a lethal or non-lethal solution for them?"

"Non-lethal," I said. "They may work for Char, but I like them. I want them disabled, not dead. I'm sure Snake and Rat can come up with some solutions for dealing with them."

Rat nodded.

"Good luck with Honor," Tiger said as I headed for the exit. "I'll let Rahbi know to expect you. Make sure she sends me some coffee."

"I'll make sure she does."

I left the conference room and headed out to inform the Director of the Light Council that he had lost a mage in the line of duty.

It was going to be a difficult day.

THIRTEEN

I rolled up to Dragonflies in the Reeds and parked just outside.

On my way out of the headquarters, I had picked up the brief Rat had provided. It was scarce on details, which was rare for Rat who prided himself on being thorough. It meant the Jane Doe had had her identity scrubbed before she went undercover.

It also meant this was an important asset for Honor.

This was going to be harder than I thought. I never enjoyed being the bearer of bad news. In some cases, it created animosity and suspicion. How did I know? Was I somehow involved in the victim's death? That sort of thing.

I sighed, grabbed the brief and stepped out of the Tank.

Dragonflies in the Reeds was a small cafe open to the public. It reminded me of a very upscale Starbucks, and was staffed by some young mages who acted as the first line of defense for the true purpose of the building that housed the cafe.

The building itself was the Central Archive and Honor's

legacy. Very few mages—and it was mostly mages who graced its interior—could visit the Central Archive directly.

Honor had set up a vetting system, whereby if you wanted access, you would reach out and leave a message. If he was feeling social that day, or you were important enough, you'd get a call back.

I fell into a different category.

The Directive, specifically Tiger and me, had assisted Honor on several occasions when the Archive had been targeted for theft and explosive renovation. A few times, we had prevented an incident without anyone noticing. Other times, we had to be somewhat proactive, thwarting the attempt violently.

In every incident, the Directive acted alone, giving Honor plausible deniability and keeping his reputation untarnished. It would raise too many questions if the Director of the Light Council was known to associate with the likes of the Directive.

It explained why I was in Dragonflies in the Reeds and not in the Central Archive proper. One of the staff nodded at me, and headed downstairs, leading me to a small supply area.

He nodded again and left me alone in the small room, closing and locking the door behind him as he exited. A section of the far wall slid to one side and Rahbi stepped into the supply room.

"Sebastian," she said warmly as she approached. "It has been too long."

"It has," I said, giving her a short hug. "Is he available?"

"For you, always," she said. "This way."

I followed her through the extensive tunnel system that led to Honor's office. After several minutes of walking, she pushed aside a wall that flashed orange as she placed her hand on it.

If anyone beside Rahbi managed to access these tunnels,

they would become hopelessly lost after the first turn. The access to Honor's office was keyed to only allow two people—Honor and Rahbi. Anyone else trying to get in this way would not even have time to question their life choices before the failsafes in the wall killed them in the attempt.

Honor took his duties as Director of the Light Council seriously, but that paled in comparison to his dedication as Archivist of the Central Archive. The only thing he valued more than life itself was the Archive.

Warm light spilled into the tunnel as one of the bookcases swung to side, revealing an expansive and sparsely furnished reception area. I always had the impression that Honor barely tolerated visitors, going out of his way to make them feel, if not unwanted, uncomfortable. On a table opposite the secret entrance, I saw a large mug of coffee calling to me.

Honor's office was on the second level of the Archive looking over the entire floor. The windows of the reception area were runed to allow visitors to look out at the main floor without being seen.

I walked over to the steaming hot mug, and looked out the reception area windows. The interior of the Central Archive reminded me of a large dojo or meditation hall, the influence no doubt due to Honor's time spent training under Master Yat, among others. There were heavy Asian influences, focused on balancing the empty space with the desks situated in the center of the floor.

Along the walls, several tiered levels contained rows and rows of books, as far as the eye could follow. All the bookcases had been runed—recently from what it seemed.

I looked down.

It was early, but even so, I could see several young mages occupying some of the tables, studying texts filled with symbols. Those would be the overachievers. On every table sat several bankers' lamps with green glass shades. Seeing them brought back the memory of my long nights at the Golden Circle studying for finals.

"The runes on the bookcases," I said. "What happened?"

Rahbi handed me the mug of hot Deathwish and nodded. She gave me a few moments to enjoy the aroma, and savor the first sip before speaking. Rahbi made some of the best coffee in the city and it was one of the reasons I appreciated my visits to Honor.

"Your cousin and his partner happened, and then the Night Warden and his apprentice," she said with a smile. "Honor felt it was safer to place proximity runes on all the bookcases as a precaution."

"Has there been an attempt—?"

"No," she said, shaking her head. "He was simply being Honor."

That I understood.

Honor bordered on obsessive-compulsive when it came to keeping Archive assets secure—not that I blamed him. He was, after all, the Archivist. It came with the position.

Rahbi stepped over to the door to Honor's office and knocked. Runes flared orange and the door clicked open. She gestured to the door and stepped back.

"He's waiting for you."

As she headed out of the reception area, I noticed that, even with the passage of time, Rahbi still moved with a relaxed lethality, a lithe grace that was beautiful and terrifying at the same time.

The rumors of her being as powerful as Honor were well-founded. I had seen her in action and it was a magnificently awe-inspiring spectacle of death and destruction.

An angry Rahbi was a dangerous Rahbi, one I hoped to never have to encounter.

I pushed the door open and waited.

FOURTEEN

Honor sat behind his desk.

He had always managed to pull off looking regal without even trying. Even without using my ability I could see wisps of his energy signature floating off his body. Different strands of violet and gold encircled him, flowing around him, and resembling miniature solar flares.

It spoke to the power he possessed.

I took a moment to admire the bookcases in his office.

The very fortified and protected bookcases in his office.

The second level of the Archive, the level currently occupied by Honor's office, was reserved for rare books and documents which were sealed behind magically enhanced glass.

If I wanted to read a rare book, it would require either Honor or Rahbi to access the case, before escorting me to a secure, compartmentalized reading room. Several of the more rare books were never allowed out of their cases, due to their age or the contents of the book.

Books of forbidden power always had a way of attracting the psychotic magic user and Honor was responsible for some of the most forbidden books in magic.

Some of the most rare and dangerous books sat in this office.

Sitting in their bookcases, behind Honor, I could see books on dark magic and entities of darkness. Not exactly what I would call light reading. Some—most—were on the acquisition of power using abilities and methods that were considered forbidden, at least forbidden by the established authorities in the magical community.

There was a reason he had been left to his own devices.

The Light and Dark Councils, NYTF, and all of the sects left him alone to oversee the Archive not because it was a boring, tedious job with long hours and no pay—although money was never an issue for Honor. It was because being the caretaker of magical books was the equivalent of painting an enormous bullseye on your back.

Everyone knew where the Central Archive was.

It was one of the first locations you learned of as a young mage. If you were an ambitious mage, morally ambiguous, willing to break any and all rules, you might consider that the fastest and easiest way to acquire unimaginable power was to steal a book from the Central Archive.

In that, you would be right.

Where you would be wrong would be in thinking you could actually pull it off. The entire Archive was ensconced in the center of a massive null field, one that Honor could activate with a thought. If you somehow made it past that, aside from the multitude of runes that acted as failsafes, you had the actual architecture of the interior designed to thwart any attempt at theft.

The Wordweavers' Corridors of Chaos would seem like a shortcut compared to the interior of the Archive with its defenses activated.

If by some minuscule chance of luck, or divine intervention, you bypassed those defenses, you would have to contend with an angry Rahbi. An angry Rahbi was a ridiculously lethal Rahbi.

If, by some wild stretch of the imagination, Rahbi failed to dispatch you into a painful oblivion, there was still Honor to contend with, at which point, it would be more merciful if you launched yourself into oblivion rather than face a determined Honor.

His power level, while never accurately measured, easily exceeded that of an Archmage. In addition to that, his title as Archivist wasn't an empty honorific. It came with a force multiplier within the walls of the Central Archive.

Which meant that however powerful he was at base, it was multiplied countless times *inside* the Central Archive. While he was inside the Archive, Honor could face off against a god, and still manage to keep the coffee in his mug undisturbed.

I still remembered that one deity, Nabu, an ancient god of wisdom and writing, who had felt entitled to borrow a book of proto-runes from Honor's office without permission.

It didn't end well.

The knowledge contained in this office was volatile, dangerous and easily abused. It made sense that the person tasked with keeping this information safe and away from those who would abuse it, was calm and laid back, slow to temper and with an easygoing way of being.

And extremely powerful.

"Come in," Honor said in his bass voice. "It's been too long, Sebastian."

I stepped through the threshold and felt the frisson of energy as it raced across my skin.

"More defensive measures?" I asked as the tingling subsided. "Someone tried to breach your office?"

"Not yet," Honor said, "I'd prefer not to wait until it happens."

It was then that I noticed the extra defensive measures. Every wall held cases of books. Even though he had dismissed my inquiries into recent attacks, his actions on the upgraded defenses spoke volumes.

The failsafes were reinforced by lethal runes, and those were, in turn, reinforced by runes that would make you beg for death after you realized your grievous error of trying to steal one of those books.

No one was reaching the books in his office and living to tell the tale.

Nothing else had changed much since my last visit. As usual, his office was mostly empty. He never kept chairs for guests in his office.

"No one stays long enough to sit, still?" I said, gesturing and creating a comfortable wingback chair. "You really do need to get out more, Honor."

He smiled and shook his head as he leaned back in his chair.

"Old habits," he said, grabbing his mug of coffee. "I'm always happy to see you, but I'm curious. It's been some time since you've paid me a visit. What brings you to the Archive? Do you need a book?"

"I'm not here for Archive business," I said, gazing at him over my cup as I took a sip. I placed the cup on the available marble coaster. "I'm here to address the status of one of your Light Council assets."

I placed the brief Rat had created on the desk.

His desk was a large, granite affair which dominated one side of his office. In the background, I could hear Concha Buika's raspy voice softly serenade me with the story of La Boheme. His meticulousness was in high gear as usual. There were no books strewn about or out of place. Every stack of paper on his desk was neatly organized and equidistant from every other stack.

The same order and organization he applied to his office, carried over into his appearance. Unlike most mages, Honor did not subscribe to the typical mageiform of the House of Zegna or Armani. He preferred to dress casually. Jeans, a crisp white shirt with the sleeves rolled up, and work boots made up his ensemble.

His hair was the only area where he allowed chaos to occur. He had let it grow out down to his shoulders, but kept his beard short. His deep brown eyes flashed with violet energy as he stared at me.

"I see," he said. "Can you clarify?"

I needed to tread carefully.

Not because I was in any personal danger.

Honor and I were more than friends. We had fought and shed blood on battlefields and the streets of this city. I had saved his life on more than one occasion, and he had done the same for me, more times than I could recount.

The danger lay in where we operated in terms of the authorities of our respective worlds. As the Director of the Light Council, he had a vast amount of authority and influence, but was hindered by the tenets of the Light Council and his position as its Director.

As for me, being the Director of the Treadwell Supernatural Directive—well, it's right there in the name, wasn't it? I only answered to the Directive and operated on the much simpler tenets of: Might makes right, only the strong survive, and justice reaches us all...eventually.

If I divulged too much, he could be forced to act as the Director of the Light Council. I needed to know how much information he possessed before sharing.

"How about *you* share and I confirm?" I said. "That way we avoid any messy entanglements."

He nodded, understanding the subtext of my statement.

"You can start with that," I continued, pointing to the brief. "I'm sure you can fill in some of the gaps."

As he read the sparse brief, I saw his expression darken.

"How accurate is this report?"

"Which part?"

"The only part that matters," he said. "Is she really dead?"

"I'm afraid so," I said. "I was on site and examined the body myself. She was completely devoid of an energy signature. I'm sorry."

"So am I," he said after a few moments. "She was one of the best operatives I had. Have you heard about a group calling themselves Umbra?"

I shared the little I knew about the organization.

He reached into one of his desk drawers and pulled out a folder, placing it on the desk, just so. He motioned for me to take it, which I did.

"This is some detailed work," I said, looking through the folder. "How long have you been after them?"

"About three months," he said. "Some of my mages have been turning up dead uptown. I sent Cat—Catherine, to infiltrate the group. They must have blown her cover somehow."

"What do you know about their leader, this Fakul Bijan?" I asked.

"Not much," he said. "He was a low level player a few years ago, no known affiliation. Disappears for about a year, and then comes back. Power level is considerably higher, and now runs this Umbra group. I'm sure he has some kind of backing, but I can't pinpoint it."

This was where I needed to be careful.

"He has an artifact," I said slowly. "One that is probably responsible for his increase in strength."

"An artifact?" Honor said, curious. "Do you know which one?"

"That would depend on who I'm speaking to right now," I

said, still measuring my words. "Am I speaking to the Director of the Light Council or the Archivist of the Central Archive?"

He leaned back and stared at me before reaching forward and grabbing his mug to take a long pull of his coffee.

"That would depend on what this artifact is and what kind of threat it presents," he said. "You know the Light Council can't allow a dangerous artifact to roam the streets of the city. Especially not in the hands of a murderer."

"I understand that, but there is more at play here," I said, pausing before speaking again. "Char."

He closed his eyes and rubbed his temple.

"Char," he said the name like a curse. "Are you certain?"

"Completely."

"How does she figure into this—you know what?" He raised a hand. "No. I don't want to know."

"Are you certain?"

"If I don't know, I don't have to arrest you, mobilize a team to shut down the Dungeon, and take her into preemptive custody."

"Do you think you can?"

"Without massive amounts of bloodshed? No."

"There is that," I said. "But you still want to know what the artifact is. Don't you?"

I knew he did. He was an archivist and that meant he was a student of all things magical. His innate and overwhelming curiosity wouldn't let him rest until I told him.

I just had to wait. It wouldn't take long.

I sat back and sipped my coffee, looking off to the side at the rare books surrounding us. Many of these books had been thought lost to time and history. It was due to Honor's efforts that they had been saved and preserved.

We may have disagreed on many things, but I did respect

what he did for the magical community by saving our past through these books.

I remained silent as he stared at me.

We had been here before, and he always lost.

In his core, there was an ever-present yawning gulf that needed to know—especially when it came to artifacts and magical tomes. It was what made him such a powerful mage and an excellent Director.

Me, on the other hand, I was comfortable with the presence of mystery and the unknown. I didn't need to know how everything worked, just that it worked the way I expected it work. My attitude used to drive him insane when we were younger.

"This is excellent coffee by the way," I said, holding up the cup after taking another sip. "Has Rahbi become more skilled at making this?"

"You win," he said, defeated. "What is it?"

"On one condition," I said, which was the other reason for my coming to see him. "If you have information on the artifact, I need it...for Goat."

"Goat?"

"Yes," I said. "He's going to try and reverse-engineer it."

"You intend on replicating this artifact?"

"No, I intend on replicating its properties."

"And you want me to help you with that?" he asked. "You know I can't."

"Then I can't share what the artifact is," I said with a shrug. It was a gambit. He could easily ask me to leave, and I would have to leave without any additional information—information that only he possessed—but it was a risk I had to take. "I understand, responsibilities and all that."

I made to stand and he held out a hand.

"Wait," he said. "What do you intend to do with the artifact?"

"Destroy it," I said. "It's too dangerous to leave out on the streets or in the hands of Char."

I kept the information about Regina's buyer to myself. That would come in handy later.

"On your word? As a mage and a Treadwell?"

Now we were stepping into serious territory.

To give my word as a mage was serious enough, and with major implications if I broke the agreement. To give my word as a Treadwell, on the name of my family, was unbreakable to me, and he knew this.

It was his turn to lean back and stare at me as he sipped.

It was my turn to pause.

He knew I would give in, the same way I knew he would surrender to his curiosity. To call my integrity into question was unacceptable, both as a mage and as a Treadwell.

We had played each other well.

"If you provide me with the information on the artifact—"

"Provided I *have* information on this artifact."

"Then on my word as a mage and a Treadwell, I will assure the artifact will be destroyed, if possible."

"And if it can't be destroyed?"

"Then I will place it in the safest location I know," I said. "I recently heard the Central Archive just upgraded its security. Will that suffice?"

He nodded, but wasn't done.

"And any replicated device or weapon with its properties is kept out of the hands of those that would use it for profit, or ill against the defenseless."

I stared at him.

He hadn't become Director by being foolish. He knew if I agreed to those terms it would bind me as well, even if I only intended to replicate the artifact's properties.

"And kept out of the hands of those that would use it for profit, or ill against the defenseless," I repeated. "Satisfied?"

"Quite," he said then took another sip of coffee before continuing. "What is the artifact?"

"The Gauntlet of Mahkah."

FIFTEEN

"You must be mistaken," Honor said, his expression grim. "That artifact has been destroyed."

"One has," I corrected. "They are a pair. One still survives and is being used by this Fakul."

"You acquired this information from a reliable source?"

"Char."

He nodded and pressed his lips together in frustration. Whatever his opinions of her as a dragon may have been, he couldn't deny the veracity of her information.

"She may be many questionable things, but when it comes to information, she's solid," he said as he reached into another desk drawer, pulled out a book, and placed it on top of the desk. "You're going to need this, then."

I looked at the book and realized it dealt with the Gauntlets of Mahkah, and Mahkah himself. I raised an eyebrow, knowing I had been outplayed.

"You knew?"

"I *guessed*," he said with a smile. "You confirmed it with the news about Cat."

"But you had this book ready?"

"I'm the Archivist of the Central Archive," he said, pushing the book toward me. "Of course I had a book ready."

"Why didn't you move against Umbra?" I asked. "You had a reasonable suspicion they were behind the deaths of your mages."

"It's not enough," he said. "At least not enough for the Light Council. You know I can't take unilateral action. Not without starting an *incident*. This is me taking action. Do *not* lose that book."

"I won't," I said, placing it inside my jacket pocket. "Can I also borrow that file on Umbra?"

"No," he said, placing a thin USB drive on the desk. "I need the actual file, but it's all there on that drive."

He had anticipated me deftly.

"Thank you," I said, taking the USB drive. "You knew I would ask."

"Archivist?" he said. "It's my job to anticipate and prepare."

"You made me swear a bond on my name," I said, staring at him in mild shock. "Why?"

"Because that gauntlet *needs* to be destroyed," he said. "It's too dangerous to exist in the wild, and I know that even if you replicate its properties, whatever you do, it won't be to kill or destroy the defenseless. The gauntlet itself, however, can be lost, stolen, or traded. I needed a guarantee before I helped you."

I wasn't offended in the least. Had our positions been reversed, I would have done the same thing. After all, I was the one that moved in the shadows, while he was the Director of the Light Council.

I smiled.

"I keep forgetting how good you are at this," I said as I stood. "It's always a pleasure to face off against you."

"And you," he said, standing as he extended a hand which

I took. "I've just had a bit more practice than you. Unlike the Directive, I have to walk in several worlds at once to maintain peace. I'm familiar with the shadows."

"I'll keep that in mind—for next time."

He nodded and Rahbi appeared at the door.

"I wish you luck, Sebastian," he said. "Try not to antagonize Char too much. She has a short temper and a long reach. You don't want to face either."

"I don't intend to," I said. "If this goes according to plan, she'll invite me to a corrective conversation at best."

"And at worst?"

"The Directive will cease to exist."

He nodded.

"Make sure your plan works, then."

"I intend to."

Rahbi led me out of the office.

SIXTEEN

Rahbi led me back to the supply room of the cafe in silence. I was about to head back up the stairs to the cafe itself when she placed a hand on my arm.

"Before you go," she said, "I thought you should know—Regina is in town."

I was curious but not surprised. Rahbi could match Rat when it came to information gathering. Very few things of import happened in the city without her—and Honor's—knowledge.

The arrival of Regina would cause ripples in the underground.

Unpleasant and violent ripples.

There were many who would be apprehensive at her arrival; those weren't a valid threat. However, there were others—individuals that wielded power—who would want nothing more than to see Regina dead, preferably after an extended session of torture first.

She had that effect on people.

"I'm aware."

"You're not the only one."

I looked back to the entrance of the tunnel we had just used.

"He knew?"

"Who do you think called Ramirez with specific instructions to call *you*? He knows," she said slowly, "more than he ever lets on. He can't act directly, but—"

"He knows *we* can," I finished, shaking my head. "He cares too much, that's his fatal flaw."

She let out a small chuckle and shook her head as I raised an eyebrow in her direction.

"Really?" she asked. "You're serious?"

"What?"

"You think you're so different?"

"Honor and I are *not* the same."

"True, most don't whisper the name of *Honor* in the shadows the way they do *Treadwell—Death's Dragon.*"

My blood ran cold at the mention of the old moniker. It brought back a rush of memories, most of them bloody and dangerous. I shook myself out of my reverie.

"I'm not that...person any longer," I said, my expression growing dark. "That was a long time ago."

"Not as long as you would like to think," she said, glancing down the tunnel. "Names take on a life of their own. He has a few he wishes he could forget."

"That doesn't make us similar."

"More similar than you think, or are willing to admit."

"I find that unlikely," I said. "Honor prefers to walk in the light. It's right there in the name of his title. Director of the *Light* Council. He's always been that way, and likely always will be."

"He knows what it means to walk in the shadows," she said, her voice serious. "You know this."

"He knows what it means to *walk* in the shadows, true," I said with a nod. "I know what it means to *live* in the darkness. They are not the same. Having shadows means there is light…somewhere. I will tell you what makes us different."

"Please do," she said with a tight smile as she rested a hand on her hip. "Illuminate me."

"There are some who think they can walk in both worlds, like he does, but what ends up happening is that the light devours them," I said. "The light is uncompromising and singular in its jealousy. It will tolerate no competition, demanding an unwavering and unswerving loyalty and dedication."

"And the shadows don't?"

"Power, real power, doesn't reside in the shadows," I continued, looking off into the tunnel. "It thrives in darkness, and it is there where it must be confronted and conquered, not from the safety of the shadows."

"The darkness has a habit of devouring those who think they can dwell in it too," she said, giving me a look. "How do you prevent that from happening?"

"You don't conquer darkness just by living in it," I said, my voice grim, "any more than you conquer the light by walking in it."

"How do *you* conquer the darkness?"

I handed her my empty mug of coffee.

"Thank you, it was delicious."

"Answer the question."

"You *know* the answer," I said. "For me, darkness is conquered by becoming more than that which you fear. By becoming the darkness itself."

She shook her head.

"That is a recipe for disaster," she said, holding my mug. "That way leads to madness and death, Sebastian."

"We all have our paths to travel," I said. "No one said our lives would be easy or filled with only sunshine and rainbows."

"True, but right now *you* are walking this path because

Honor stepped into the shadows and shone a light on you and your Directive," she said. "At great risk to himself, I might add."

"That was out of character for him," I said with a nod. "I underestimated him."

"Most do, but he likes and respects you," she said, "He gave you the book?"

"Yes, that was unexpected."

"That's Honor. Keep that book safe and don't let Regina get that gauntlet. If her buyer acquires that artifact, it would be worse than giving it to Char."

"Do you know who the buyer is?"

Rahbi smiled at me and shook her head.

"You'll find out soon enough."

"Wouldn't it be easier if you just told me?"

"It would, but then you wouldn't be able to act later," she said. "It's better she tells you."

"You think Regina is going to tell me?" I said. "We must be discussing different people. The Regina I know would never divulge the identity of her buyer. It's how she has remained alive for so long. She doesn't discuss her clients."

"Don't be so sure," Rahbi said. "Everyone changes."

"I still think you should—"

"Time for you to go," she said, cutting me off and heading back into the tunnel. "We'll be watching, and I hope you pull off whatever it is you're up to this time."

"So do I."

The next moment, she and the entrance to the tunnel were gone.

I left Dragonflies in the Reeds and stepped outside.

This trip to Honor had given rise to more questions than answers, typical of my trips to the Central Archive. How did Honor know Regina was back in the city? More importantly, how did he know who her client was? Why wouldn't he share that information with me?

For a brief moment I contemplated going back and asking him, but it was futile. For one, he was vastly stronger than me; it wasn't like I could force him to answer me. He was also incredibly stubborn and would refuse to answer me on principle alone.

I had played this game before. I would have to uncover the answers elsewhere. The fact the Honor knew meant that the answers were accessible; I just had to ask the wrong people the right questions.

The Tank waited for me, an ominous sliver of matte black sitting in the early morning sun. Pedestrians unconsciously gave it a wide berth, due to the aversion runes Cecil had used on it.

I placed my hand on its surface and it unlocked with a soft rumble. I seriously questioned Cecil's mental state when he created these vehicles of obvious and overt menace.

The term mad genius came to mind as I sat behind the wheel and started the engine. I pressed a button on the dash and activated the hands-free phone function.

"Treadwell Supernatural Directive," Rabbit said in her receptionist voice. "We walk the shadows, so you can enjoy the light. How may I direct your call?"

She knew that I knew that she knew who was calling before she connected the call. Her little slogans were designed to nudge me into hiring an actual receptionist. I just hadn't gotten around to it.

"I like that one," I said as I drove away. "How goes the receptionist search? Any applicants?"

"Not yet," she said, the frustration creeping into her voice. "Do you have to be so honest?"

"I prefer to call it being straightforward," I said, merging into traffic. "The position comes with a particular set of risks."

"Then hire someone who can handle the risks," she answered. "I mean, that's a no-brainer."

"That's exactly what you were tasked with," I said, noticing the rune-covered black van in my rear-view mirror. "Of course, if you're finding the assignment too difficult, I could always ask Rat or Tiger—"

"Are you mad?" Rabbit shot back. "Rat will just hire some creepy ninja-receptionist. And Tiger? Are you out of your mind? You think letting Tiger hire the new receptionist is a good or safe idea?"

It was neither.

"Then you'll handle it?" I asked, smiling. "Make sure the new applicants have a decent amount of ability and are aware of the risks. I'd prefer not to have a dead receptionist inside of a week, if we can help it. Oh, and please make sure the psych evaluation is done. The last receptionist didn't handle Tiger dismantling that ogre too well."

"The ogre was trying to kill us," Rabbit clarified, "and the receptionist too."

"I'm aware of the context—having an ogre bisected before your eyes is not a common occurrence. The receptionist didn't take it too well, but I trust her replacement will be made of sterner stuff."

"I know what I need to do," she groused. "Who do you want to speak to, *Director?*"

"Connect me to Tiger, please," I said with a small chuckle. "I have every confidence in you getting us a new receptionist."

"You'll accept anyone I choose, right?" she sounded dangerously optimistic all of a sudden. "As long as they meet the criteria and know the risks, right?"

"Yes...as long as they meet the criteria and understand the risks," I said warily. "Do you have someone in mind?"

"I might," she said cheerily. "Connecting you now."

Her sudden change in mood worried me, but I had larger concerns to focus on in the moment.

"How's Honor?" Tiger said a moment later. "Still buried in his books?"

"You know him," I said. "He did provide some assistance." I glanced down at the book next to me. "We may have some more research material for Goat."

"Really?" she said. "I'm surprised he didn't give you the 'My hands are tied, because the Light Council is pure and unsullied, and I can't possibly step into the darkness to help you' speech."

"It was close to something like that," I said, watching the van in my rear-view. "He did provide me with important information regarding the gauntlet, and made it a point to let me know Regina is in town."

"Like a goddamn plague of the apocalypse," Tiger said and let out a long breath. "You should really just let me retire her."

"We can't afford the collateral damage that would incur."

"Fine. Is his Highness the Librarian of Light going to get involved...directly, I mean?"

"It's Honor."

"I'll take that as a no."

"He does recognize how dangerous the artifact is," I said, watching my tail turn off on a side street. "I have a tail."

"Any idea who it could be?" she asked, and I heard her voice grow distant as she checked her phone. "You're heading into the park?"

"No idea who it is. Black van, covered in runes," I said, glancing in the now empty rear-view mirror. "They're trying to hide and failing. If I had to guess, I'd say our new friends from Umbra. The signature on the van seems familiar."

"Familiar how?" she asked. "Familiar, 'you've seen it before', or familiar 'someone who's tried to kill you used these runes before'?"

"The former," I said. "I'm going to try and lead them to the west side. I should be able to lose them near the piers, before heading uptown."

"I can be there in ten."

"No, I have this under control," I said as the van returned to my rear-view mirror. "I'm sure they just want to have a cordial conversation."

"Sure, and I'm known for my easygoing and welcoming nature," she snapped. "What do you want me to do while you're being ambushed?"

"I'm sending over the file Honor gave me on Umbra," I said, inserting the thin USB drive into a port in the dash. "This should help Rat locate their base of operations. Once he disseminates the information, I need you to—"

I never did manage to finish that sentence.

I was so focused on the tail in my rear-view mirror that I had failed to notice the second van which rammed into the driver side of the Tank. I had just crossed the intersection of Greenwich and Laight Streets.

The driver of the second van had built up considerable speed before ramming into me. I imagined the purpose was to crush the Tank and end my life on impact.

There was a reason this vehicle was dubbed the Tank.

Cecil had used a base 1966 Lincoln Continental for the Tank.

The body, along with all of the glass, had been runically reinforced. At the moment of impact, orange-red runes flared inside the Tank, providing a cushion of energy which displaced the brunt of the impact along the entire chassis.

The impact had forcefully shoved the Tank several feet sideways, much to the surprise of the van driver. The van, on the other hand, had been totaled.

The entire front of the vehicle had crumpled as if it had slammed into a steel wall at speed, which, technically was accurate. The impact sent the driver sailing past the hood of the Tank, as his head shattered the van's windshield on his impromptu emergency flight.

He landed and rolled for a few feet before coming to a final stop. From the pool of blood forming around his body, I doubted he survived the collision.

Two more vans rolled to my location, blocking off any exit. At this hour, the streets would be deserted. Two blocks away to the west and straight ahead, I could see Pier 26 and the Hudson River.

Several men jumped out of the vans.

Tiger was yelling over the phone. I did a quick scan to make sure nothing was broken, and gave Cecil a silent heartfelt thanks for his excellence in rune work. The last thing I heard from Tiger was her informing me that she was on her way and to stay put.

There would be no dissuading her, so I ended the call without replying. I was jarred, but functional and getting steadily angrier by the second.

How did they find me?

I slowly opened the door to the unscathed Tank and stepped out.

SEVENTEEN

There were at least ten low-level mages, with one moderately powered mage acting as the leader. The leader radiated a fairly impressive energy signature, equal to the one Michael possessed.

But there was something off.

All of their energy signatures fluctuated from low threat to considerable threat levels every few seconds. I had never seen anything like it, so I kept my distance while I evaluated what I was facing.

"Sebastian Treadwell," the leader said as he approached me. "It truly is an honor."

"And you are?"

I gauged the distance between us, as more men piled out of the vans which were either larger on the inside than appearances let on, or had some kind of portal allowing them transport to this location.

The leader gave me a short bow with plenty of flourish.

"I am Fakul Bijan."

It was a lie—of sorts.

The man approaching me was a mid-level mage. However,

the mage controlling his body remotely was formidable in his signature. The man stopped about fifteen feet away.

I let my vision shift in spectrum and saw the thin, violet tethers attached to all of the mages. The tethers all trailed uptown, an intricate web of energy that led to whoever controlled these mages.

I had an idea where the tethers ended, but I had never seen such an extensive puppeteer cast. The gauntlet must have enhanced Fakul's inherent energy.

Puppeteers were a class of mages that used magical tethers to control inanimate dolls as weapons. The tethers imbued the dolls with energy and volition, making them dangerous and lethal opponents in the hand of an accomplished Puppeteer.

Fakul had violated the basic and most important tenet of the Puppeteers: never use a human as a doll. It destroyed the human's mind, body, and psyche, rendering them insane and killing them in the process.

The process of controlling them drained the human's life at an accelerated pace. Dolls never lasted long; the power used to create and control them made it a short-lived experience in more ways than one.

The fact that Fakul could control human mages spoke to the power of the gauntlet. Alone, even controlling one human would be taxing to all except a highest level Puppeteer. To control so many, meant his power was beyond imagining.

By the time all the men had exited the vans, I was facing twenty low-level mages all dressed in black suits, wielding bludgeons—heavy rigid sticks, with pointed ends. The sticks were covered with dull, pulsing red runes, and looked fairly dangerous.

Fakul's proxy held his stick in front of him, leaning slightly forward, and resting some of his weight on it as he stared at me.

"To what do I owe the honor?" I asked, quickly glancing around to make sure none of the men tried a flanking maneuver. "Why the puppets?"

"No need to take unnecessary risks," Fakul's puppet said, shifting to the side in a herky-jerky manner which seemed anatomically wrong on so many levels. "I wanted to see if you were really the threat the rumors say you are."

"It doesn't pay to listen to rumors," I said. "They're mostly lies and exaggerations."

"Why are you pursuing me?" Fakul asked. "I pose no threat to you."

"You killed someone," I said, keeping my anger under control. "A young woman."

"You are going to need to be more specific," Fakul said with a laugh. "I've killed many men...and women."

"Somehow that doesn't surprise me," I said. "I need the gauntlet."

"Gauntlet? What gauntlet?"

His response was too sudden, and the eyes of the puppet regained clarity for a few seconds, meaning Fakul's hold over him had momentarily slipped. An expression of fear, uncertainty and confusion crossed the puppet's face, all in the space of a second.

I had shaken him.

"The one you are using to increase your power and control these puppets," I said, materializing my blades. I knew where this was going, and while I didn't want to kill these mages, I doubted they had any reservations about ending my life. "The Gauntlet of Mahkah."

"I see," he said, raising his stick. It flared a bright red before he brought it down hard, burying the pointed end in the cobblestone street. "Kill him."

Even though these puppets were mages, they were unable to use their abilities while under Fakul's control, hence the rune-covered bludgeons. Two puppets closed on me, approaching me from opposite sides with that staggering stop-and-go motion that unnerved me.

They were surprisingly fast for puppets—one of the advantages of using humans—and swung their bludgeons in my direction. I jumped to the side and slashed at the head of the puppet closest to me.

He ducked down as I expected and I reversed the attack, slashing at the tethers that connected him to Fakul. He fell to the floor and began convulsing as I cut the tethers.

The second puppet swung his bludgeon which I easily sidestepped. I didn't sever the tethers because I realized what Fakul had done. He had connected the tethers to their life-force.

If I severed the tethers, they would die too, but I couldn't evade them forever. One or two were manageable; nineteen was about eighteen too many.

"You can't win," Fakul said. "My dolls will kill you."

"Unless I sever them first," I said. "But you've thought of that, haven't you?"

"Of course," Fakul answered. "These men are Umbra. They live and die to serve me. Sever the tethers, and they will fulfill their purpose."

"Wonderful. A delusional megalomaniac," I said mostly to myself. "This day just keeps getting better."

"I am not delusional," Fakul said. "I have a vision and a purpose. Umbra will allow me to achieve my goals. These men understand what it means to sacrifice for greatness."

"As long as they're the ones doing the sacrificing, correct?"

More puppets were closing on me. I was running out of time.

I dodged several swipes and moved back in an attempt to get back to the Tank. Several puppets had surrounded it, blocking my path. Things were getting ugly fast.

I absorbed my blades and picked up the bludgeon of the dead puppet. If they were unconscious, Fakul couldn't control them. I would have to incapacitate them and avoid getting my skull bashed in while I was doing so.

"You think you can disable them all?" Fakul asked. "You, alone?"

"I've faced worse odds," I said, blocking a bludgeon and ducking another as I slammed a knife-hand into the neck of another puppet, dropping him as he fell to the floor unconscious.

"You still don't understand the gravity of your situation," Fakul said as some of the puppets drew blades. "These are chaff. They only have one purpose: to end your life. Failure to do so means their lives are forfeit."

The puppet I had downed without severing the tether began to convulse. A few seconds later he too was dead.

"You bastard," I said, then noticed that the bludgeon the mid-level mage held was glowing brighter than the others. "You send others to die for you while you hide."

"It is their lot to die, while mine is to lead and usher in a new age," Fakul said. "There is no escape for you."

"I will find you," I said, moving forward to the mid-level mage. "And I will end you."

"You will try and you will fail," the Fakul puppet said, raising his bludgeon. "To me!"

I tried closing the gap, narrowly avoiding several of the puppets. One of them stepped close to me and slashed at my leg, diverting my attention for a brief second.

I sensed the energy build up from the Fakul puppet and dropped to the ground as an orb sailed past me and crashed into a puppet behind me, disintegrating him where he stood.

Obliteration orbs.

The rest of the puppets were closing in on the Fakul puppet's location.

I felt another surge of power and rolled to the side only to witness the horrific deaths of the mage puppets as their life-force was siphoned into the Fakul puppet, who had gone from mid-level mage to major threat in the space of a few seconds.

The bludgeon in his hand pulsed a bright red as all of the mages dropped where they stood and convulsed for a few seconds before becoming still and lifeless.

"You killed them all."

Fakul laughed.

"No, not all," he said. "I left you one. He is stronger than you and will be your death."

I looked around at the dead mages.

"I *will* stop you, even if it's with my last breath," I said. "I will see you breathe your last."

Fakul laughed again.

"You will not stand in my way," Fakul said. "Umbra will be victorious. I will be victorious." There was a brief pause as the puppet's eyes rolled back in his head, and he turned his face upward. "Do you hear my voice, Omar?"

The mage nodded.

"I hear your voice, my Lord," Omar said, his voice distant. "What is your wish?"

There was no way this could end well.

"Do you see the enemy?" Fakul continued. "He would stand in my way, in the way of greatness for Umbra. You will not let this happen. I have given you power. Power to rise above the others. Power to destroy all who would stand against me."

Omar's head snapped down and he opened his eyes, looking directly at me.

Bloody hell.

"Power to rise," Omar repeated, his eyes focused and his voice hollow. "Power to destroy."

"You will stop him," Fakul said. "You will end his life even if it costs you your own."

"I will end his life."

"Show him the error of his ways. Embrace him with the truth that is Umbra," Fakul commanded. "Act with haste. As the lightning bolt strikes without warning, strike down our enemy and show him no mercy."

"For the glory of Lord Fakul," he said. "For the glory of Umbra."

"Goodbye, Treadwell," Fakul said. "I must say the rumors were greatly exaggerated. I expected more."

"Sorry to disappoint," I said. "Why don't you come and see me yourself instead of sending puppets? I'm sure I can summon up something that will impress your twisted mind."

"Omar will make sure that is not necessary," Fakul said. "He will not fail me."

"You right bast—"

Something glimmered in Omar's eyes before they went dead. Fakul was gone, but Omar was still alive, and glaring at me.

"Omar, you don't need to do this," I said, holding the bludgeon in my hand. "You can resist him. Take back control of your mind. You don't belong to him."

"I belong to Lord Fakul, body and soul," Omar said, correcting me. "He is my Lord and I am his willing servant. You will realize the truth before the end."

He gripped his bludgeon tighter and rushed at me.

EIGHTEEN

I blocked the initial attack as Omar forced me back several steps.

He wasn't overly large, but whatever power Fakul had infused in him multiplied his strength several times over. He swung the bludgeon at my head, forcing me to duck.

With a twist of the top section, the bludgeon produced a long rune-covered blade from the bottom.

"You've got to be joking. Seriously?" I said, moving back out of range as I hefted the bludgeon I held and tried to find the release for a blade. Apparently only Omar's bludgeon was a blade-holding model. "Of course, figures."

I parried a thrust and deflected a horizontal slash. Omar retracted his stick and swung upward, cutting my stick in half and rendering it useless.

Clearly, Omar had the much upgraded, steel-core bludgeon, while I wielded a stick with the strength of balsa wood. I tossed the useless pieces away and materialized my blades in time to redirect another thrust.

With each strike, I noticed the runes on Omar's stick gradually getting brighter. Fakul's words were nagging at me in the back of my mind, but I was too busy trying not to get skewered or smashed in the head to pay them much mind at the moment.

For someone who had been brainwashed and controlled, Omar was moving with incredible dexterity. His strikes were disproportionately powerful, causing me to lose my footing several times as I evaded his attacks.

All the while, the runes on his stick increased in intensity.

He swung the stick at my legs, redirecting his attack at the last second and aiming for my head. I ducked into a fist which sent me sprawling. I scrambled to my feet and realized I had ended up next to the Tank.

I had options.

I could jump into the Tank and evacuate, but there was a chance Omar would go on a rampage, killing innocents. I could get in the Tank and tap him lightly with it, causing him to embrace unconsciousness. The chances of that ending in his death were too high to risk, however.

I scrapped the escape plan.

I wanted him alive, if at all possible. He was still tethered and I could follow that tether to Fakul. That was the best possible plan. The only downside was that it meant fighting Omar into submission, but not unconsciousness, especially now that Fakul had left his body.

That was going to be easier said than done.

"Listen to me, Omar," I said, moving to the side as he stabbed where I'd stood a second earlier and hit the Tank, leaving it unscathed. "You can fight this."

I backed up, drawing him closer.

He swung his stick at my head and I ducked under the attack and slashed at his leg. His clothing erupted with red runes as I struck. It didn't stop me from cutting him— kamikira blades were designed to cut through everything— but it threw me off for half a second.

It was half-a-second too long; he drove a fist into the side of my head. I bounced off the Tank and into a kick aimed at my midsection. I barely managed to avoid the brunt of the impact, taking the kick on my side instead of my abdomen.

It still knocked the wind out of me as I rolled back and tried to catch my breath. He rushed me and slammed into my chest, holding the bludgeon in front of him. We crashed to the ground and rolled as he ended up behind me. He tried to pull the stick across my neck, but I managed to get an arm in between the stick and my throat.

The runes kept getting brighter, and Fakul's words which had been simmering in the back of my mind suddenly came to the forefront of my consciousness: *Act with haste. As the lightning bolt strikes without warning, strike down our enemy and show him no mercy.*

I immediately had the sudden and dire need to put some distance between Omar and me. I rolled to the side, poised to strike with my blades when a blast hit us both, sending us flying.

A second blast hit me and sent me to the right, bouncing me off the Tank again, while Omar sailed to the left. Dazed and confused, I had lost all sense of direction when a pair of hands grabbed me roughly, pulling me into the Tank.

I turned in time to see Omar running towards me. The stick in his hand was too bright to look at as he closed the distance. He had reached the Tank when the bludgeon in his hand detonated. All of the runes inside the Tank flared a bright orange as the explosion shoved it back several feet.

The windshield darkened as the energy bloomed with a flash, blinding me and obscuring everything. When I could see again, the windows had become transparent. I saw the vans had become molten slag, resembling anything but vehicular transport. The crater in the middle of the street was still smoking, and there was no sign of Omar or the rest of the mage puppets.

"I'm really glad Cecil doesn't scrimp on his runework," Tiger said beside me as the sound of sirens could be heard in the distance. "What the hell was that? You know what? Nevermind that right now. I think you need to drive away from the scene of the explosion."

"Huh? What?" I said, my brain still trying to process what had happened. "Why are you here?"

She shoved open her door and ran over to my side, pulling me out and helping me into the rear. I sat back and winced as she slammed the door closed.

"Like we have time for a chat," she said with a grumble. "NYTF is going to be all over this, and we can't be here when they arrive. How hard did you hit your head?"

I put a hand to the back of my head and it came away bloody.

"Fairly hard it seems," I said, holding up my hand. "Did you do this?"

"Shit," she said and sped away from the crater. "Okay, sit still and do not go to sleep. Tell me what happened."

"Fakul happened."

"That tells me nothing," she snapped. I felt my vision go hazy and then a sudden pain in my face brought my vision into crisp focus. "Hey! Stay with me!"

"What?" I said, pushing her hand away. "What is it?"

"Tell me what happened," she said, driving across the city. "Give me the details. Step by step. C'mon, work that methodical brain of yours. The last thing I heard, you had a tail."

"A tail, yes," I said as it came back to me. "The black vans I had seen uptown where I encountered Umbra's men. Near the mage ronin territory."

"Good, what happened after that?"

I closed my eyes to gather my thoughts, but another slap crashed across my cheek.

"That was completely unnecessary," I said, rubbing my face. "I was sorting my thoughts."

"Sort them with your eyes open."

"If I don't have a concussion already, your slap therapy is going to give me one," I snapped, moving my jaw to make sure it wasn't broken. "Where are you going?"

"Haven," she said, and I shook my head. "It's the best—"

"No," I said. "Roxanne is busy and I'd rather not involve...family."

"She's not going to tell *him,*" Tiger said somewhat reluctantly. "Is she?"

"She will find herself forced to. Tristan is family," I said as I became more lucid. "If I'm injured, she will feel it's her duty to inform my next of kin. Roxanne may operate outside of the rules on occasion, but she is the Director of Haven. She can't ignore them completely."

"Ugh," Tiger said. "Where do you want me to take you?"

"Take me to Ivory."

She gave me a quick glance which spoke volumes.

"The Tower...are you certain?" she asked, her voice wary. "Haven would be—"

"Ivory," I said, leaving no room for argument. "She is an advanced healer, and will see me immediately."

"Only because she has some weird fascination with you," Tiger said, turning the car around and heading uptown. "There are other healers in the city you know. Some are actually less creepy than Ivory."

"Few that are as good as Ivory," I said. "She won't feel compelled to contact Tristan. She is a trusted and reliable source."

"Ivory is also an ifrit," Tiger protested. "In some places, that's considered a demon."

"Who are we to judge her?" I said. "She keeps a low profile and rather than venture out and kill people, she helps them. I'd say that's a plus for us."

"There is that," Tiger conceded. "Not everyone wants to go to Haven."

"The fact that Haven's treatment wing lies above a detention area may be something of a deterrent," I said. "Especially to those who would prefer to remain outside the accepted norms of the Councils or NYTF."

"This is risky," Tiger said, shaking her head. "Messing with demons always ends badly. And her Tower gives me a headache."

"We are not 'messing' with her," I said. "Ivory is a friend. She provides a valuable service, and she may be the only one who can help us against Fakul and that gauntlet."

"That doesn't change the fact that seeing her is a risk."

"A calculated risk, and I needed to see her anyway," I said, resting my head back, but keeping my eyes open. "Fakul is a Puppeteer."

"Is that what was attacking you?" she asked. "One of his puppets?"

"A human mage puppet."

"A human?" she said, incredulous. "Wouldn't that violate—?"

"Yes," I said. "I was going to see Ivory in any case. Now it seems I *need* to see her."

"A human puppet," Tiger said, her voice low. "But those bodies...?"

"He treats them as expendable tools," I said, measuring my words carefully. Tiger still hadn't processed the Jane Doe, and hearing that Fakul was enslaving and discarding mages wasn't going to make her feel any better. "He uses the gauntlet to control them. Somehow it alters their thought process and makes them slaves to his will."

"He siphons them?" she said, gripping the wheel of the Tank tighter. "He killed *all* of them?"

"Yes," I said. "The last mage had been given the life-force of the other mages before detonating. Fakul was able to do this remotely. When I attempted to sever the connection, they would die."

"Because of the gauntlet."

"Yes," I said. "It appears to allow the user to manipulate the minds of its targets, imparting them with power or siphoning their ability."

"And why do you need to see Ivory?"

"She may have an artifact that can deal with the siphoning aspect of the gauntlet," I said. "I don't relish the idea of facing Fakul without some way of neutralizing the siphoning."

"Are you sure she has some anti-siphon artifact?"

"That we will have access to? Fairly certain," I said. "The only other entity would be Char, and considering she requested I *give* her the gauntlet, I'm disinclined to visit her and ask for a counter to its ability."

"That almost sounds like you don't trust the dragon."

"I respect Char, but trust? That would be foolish and suicidal. The Dungeon is not a viable option right now."

"Not to mention my temporary ban."

"Well, there is that as well," I said. "I don't know how you manage to antagonize so many people on a regular basis."

"It's my gift."

I moved my hand to the wound on my head. I was still bleeding, just not as much as earlier. I would have to cast healing runes until we arrived at Ivory's Tower.

"I just had the Tank detailed," she said. "Do not start bleeding all over the interior."

"I'll try to minimize the bleeding," I said. "Did Rat get the information?"

"He did, he's working on it," she said, concern lacing her voice. "Are you sure you want to see her?"

"No choice," I said, rubbing a temple to fend off the impending headache. "It's either Ivory or Char, and you are currently persona non grata at the Dungeon."

"That was not my fault," she said, before voicing her true worry. "Ivory is dangerous and always creeps me out. Those eyes of hers are wrong."

"Don't read too much into it," I said, gesturing and casting golden healing runes on my body. "Ivory creeps everyone out."

NINETEEN

She drove for a few more minutes before arriving at 220 Central Park South, Ivory's home near the Park. Her tower sat on West 58th Street between Broadway and 7th Avenue. At seventy stories, it was an imposing property.

The rumor was that Ivory owned the entire building. It wasn't out of the realm of possibility. I was certain she had accrued a staggering amount of wealth over her years of existence.

Ivory was probably as old, if not older than Char.

She catered to a very select clientele, most whom lived and operated outside of the accepted norms of the magical community. Even within the Directive, few knew of my true involvement with Ivory.

I had been present to her summoning by a sorcerer with, let's say, less than honorable intentions. He had planned on using Ivory as a weapon against his enemies.

He had made the fatal error of using borrowed power to summon her; it cost him his life once she discovered the truth. I had the means to dispatch her back to her domain, but we had reached an agreement.

I liked to think it was a mutually beneficial arrangement.

Tiger parked the Tank outside the building. The aversion runes Cecil had placed on the vehicle ensured it would be there when we returned. We entered the lobby of the building and made our way to the penthouse elevators.

I placed my hand on a section of the wall next to the elevator doors which whispered open with a sigh. Ivory lived on the top five floors of the building. The lower three floors were a state-of-the-art medical facility, while the upper two served as her living quarters.

We stepped into the elevator.

There was no panel, no buttons, nothing to designate the elevator's destination. The only way to access this elevator was having a specific rune which only Ivory could impart.

She never had unwanted visitors.

Those who needed her services paid a premium for them. In return, she would do her best to treat the injury—usually magical in nature—or provide off-plane assistance when needed or warranted.

The doors sighed closed, and bright white and blue runes covered the interior of the elevator. There was a momentary sensation of upward motion and then a sudden stillness. Several seconds later, the doors opened, and we stepped out onto the lower level of the medical facility.

Everything was modern and clean, with personnel moving about their designated duties. It appeared to be like any other hospital, if you overlooked the faintly glowing white runes in the walls, floors, and ceilings.

All of the staff wore blue-accented white uniforms, with the exception of the large security personnel stationed prominently at key locations throughout the floor.

I had it on good authority that the security for Ivory's Tower consisted of Rakshasi who had served Ivory for centuries. I had never seen one of her security without their golden face coverings, so I had no way to determine the authenticity of the rumor.

Suffice to say, having eight-foot security guards standing around the floor, each armed with a very large blade strapped to their back, in addition to the several blades in sheaths along their legs, made the medical facility in the Tower a very peaceful place.

If they were really Rakshasi, they were formidable and lethal fighters, not to mention cunning and highly intelligent. I hoped never to see them in action.

We had taken a step into the reception area when Ivory appeared in front of me. She made it a point to personally greet every patient, and her expression of surprise softened when she saw me.

Her eyes were her most off-putting feature. They were pitch-black with flecks of gold in them. When she was angry, the gold would be replaced with bright red flames.

It was as disturbing as it sounds. No one ever went out of their way to make Ivory upset. She wore a deep indigo set of rune-covered scrubs and a matching scrub cap. She may have had immense power and owned the facility, but she believed on being hands-on in the care of her patients.

"Sebastian," she said and looked at Tiger as she motioned to a nurse for a wheel chair. "Tiger, welcome. How serious is this?"

"You're going to have to tell me," Tiger said. "When I arrived on the scene, he was getting his ass kicked all over the place."

Ivory smiled as she took the wheelchair from the nurse and began pushing me down a corridor.

"I have missed speaking with you Tiger," Ivory said. "Is that your official diagnosis?"

"I saw him bounce off the Tank and then the ground, and he almost got himself blasted into little Sebastian particles."

"You've been keeping busy, I see," Ivory said, glancing down at me. "Let's get you looked at, and then we can determine the extent of the damage."

"I'm fine," I said. "It's just a bump on the head."

She sniffed the air and shook her head.

"The blood loss says different," she said as she wheeled me into a room. "You took precautions, I see, with a healing cast."

I nodded.

"You know it's not my strong suit."

"Nor is avoiding damage, apparently," she said, feeling the back of my head. "What were you fighting?"

She stood in front of me and shone a low-beam flashlight into my eyes from the outer edge inward. She repeated the process in both my eyes.

"A puppet," I said. "A human puppet."

She flexed her jaw at my words.

"Human puppets are a violation of the cast," she said, her voice tight with anger. "Are you certain they were human?"

"Yes," I said. "They were being controlled against their will."

"No one volunteers to be a human puppet, Sebastian," she said, putting the flashlight away. "You have a mild concussion."

"Does he have brain damage?" Tiger asked. "I'm pretty sure he has brain damage."

"I don't sense any intracranial pressure," Ivory said, placing her hands on my head. "If he has brain damage, it occurred prior to today's activities."

"Hmm, that's also a possibility," Tiger said. "Unlikely to be a genetic cause though."

"Thank you, Doctor Tiger," I said with a glance at her. "I'm not here because of the injury, well not only the injury."

"Really? Why *are* you here?"

"The mage controlling the puppets was using an artifact."

The silence stretched out as Ivory placed both hands on the back of my head and let energy flow through her. A few moments later, I felt excellent as the headache subsided then disappeared.

"That took care of the concussion," she said, taking a seat on a stool near a computer station. "I need you not to engage in physical activity for 48 hours, limit exposure to bright lights, and no loud noises or explosions."

"Does Tiger count as a loud noise?"

"I'm sensing definite brain damage," Tiger replied with a glare. "Imminent even."

"It will help your recovery," Ivory said, ignoring Tiger's not-so-subtle threat. "Do you think you can manage this?"

"Unlikely," I said, shaking my head. "I'm in the middle of this."

"I didn't think so," she said. "At the very least, avoid head blows for the next few days. The cast I placed on you should manage the rest. Now, you mentioned an artifact?"

"I did," I said. "What do you know about the Gauntlets of Mahkah?"

"Powerful siphons able to drain magical energy from a target and impart the captured energy to another," she said. "They were also used to heighten the latent energy of the user as a type of force multiplier. It's my understanding they were destroyed."

"One of them was," I said. "It appears one is still functional."

"And you think this puppeteer mage is using it?"

"I do," I said. "Do you have anything that would counter a siphon?"

Ivory grew pensive for a few moments.

"That depends."

"On?"

"How much of your life you are willing to risk."

TWENTY

"How much would I need to risk to prevent being siphoned?"

"A substantial amount," she said. "Have you ever heard of the theory of Vanko's Vortex?"

"Yes. The theoretical method of capturing a void vortex and maintaining it in a form of stasis," I said. "But that's only a thought exercise. No one has been able to successfully execute that cast. It always fell apart due to instability."

"Correct; it always fell apart because the vortex would prove too powerful for any form of containment," Ivory said. "That was, until recently."

"Recently? How recently?"

"Several decades now."

"Several decades?" I asked, surprised. "How is it that this hasn't become common knowledge in the magical community?"

"You are aware what a void vortex is?" Ivory asked, giving me an incredulous look. "You realize how dangerous a vortex can be?

"Of course, I'm aware," I said. "However, this is a significant breakthrough. Why has it been kept secret?"

"Weaponizing the power of a void vortex..." Ivory started slowly, "you really think this information should be common knowledge?"

"Like I said, brain damage," Tiger chimed in. "Why not throw in a pair of runic nuclear bombs to go with the vortex? It would be used as a *weapon*. Can you stop a void vortex?"

"I've never had the necessity to attempt it," I said. "But what does a void vortex have to do with stopping a siphon?"

"Not stopping, redirecting," Ivory said and gestured, opening a portal next to her. She looked into the portal and thrust an arm into it. "One moment."

She rummaged through the portal for close to a minute before removing a small violet pendant attached to a silver chain. The pendant was shaped in the form of a whirlpool and exuded an enormous energy signature.

"What is that?" I said, eyeing the pendant warily. "It possesses an intense energy signature."

"It should," she said. "It's a vortex isolator."

"A what?" I asked in disbelief. "Are you saying that thing can contain a void vortex?"

"Yes, for a short time," Ivory said. "Remember when I asked you how much of your life you are willing to risk?"

"I do, yes."

"The gauntlet works on contact, if I remember the details correctly," she said. "In order to disable the siphon, you would cast a void vortex and isolate it, capturing it in this pendant, which is closer to a pocket dimension."

"And then what?"

"When the mage tries to siphon you—"

"It begins to siphon the vortex instead."

Ivory nodded.

"You are both insane," Tiger said. "Do you know how much damage an uncontrolled void vortex can do?"

"I am aware," Ivory said. "This is, however, one of the best ways to counter a siphon."

"Not exactly safe," Tiger said.

"I didn't say one of the safest, I said one of the best."

"How long can the isolator hold the vortex?" I asked. "How much time am I working with?"

"That I don't know," Ivory said. "I do know the isolator works though, since I tested it when I first discovered it. For obvious reasons, I didn't test the outer limits of its containment."

"Obvious reasons," Tiger repeated while looking at me. "Like not destroying the plane."

"That would be one, yes," Ivory admitted. "Vortices have a habit of being unpredictable and unstable, but the isolator *can* stop a siphon effectively and disable the gauntlet."

"By essentially overloading it," I said. "It would require casting a vortex and getting in proximity of the gauntlet."

"Not proximity. Contact," Tiger clarified. "That bastard would have to touch you with it. Is that what you want? If this goes wrong, he'll drain you dry."

"What I want is to stop Fakul from creating another Jane Doe," I said, my voice hard. "I want him to stop creating, using, and killing human puppets. I want him to pay for what he's done. That's what *I* want. What do you want?"

"I want the same things," Tiger shot back, "without risking your life in the process."

I took the isolator and placed it around my neck.

"No one said this was going to be easy," I said. "You know our lives by now. When has easy ever been part of that equation?"

"Never," Tiger grumbled and looked at Ivory. "How does it work? Give it to me forwards, backwards and sideways. We can't afford to make a mistake with this thing."

Ivory walked us through the process.

For the first time in a long time, I felt the cold hand of death gently caress my skin. If this went wrong, Fakul would not only end my life, he would hold the power of both the gauntlet and a void vortex in his hands.

Nothing and no one would be able to stop him.

TWENTY-ONE

"This is insane," Tiger said as we drove away from Ivory's Tower. "There are too many variables, too many things can go wrong."

"I don't see an alternative, do you?"

"Sure, we storm Umbra's HQ and drive a blade through Fakul's chest—even better, a round between his eyes," she said, the rage bubbling to the surface. "We end that bastard clean, no risking the plane or the entire population of the city, if something goes wrong."

"I'm not advocating for risking the plane or the population," I said as I switched lanes between traffic. "I just don't think either of those strategies are sound."

"Why not?"

"He will surround himself with puppets, most of whom will be set to detonate," I said, extrapolating from the earlier fight. "If I were Fakul, I would make sure I had some insurance plan in place, in the event of my death."

"I know this sounds cold," Tiger said, "but his puppets made their choice when they joined him. I know there are no acceptable losses, but we're gambling with the lives of the millions of people in this city. Don't you think?"

"I don't think we can save them after they become puppets," I said. "The problem is we don't know how many of them he has, and where they may be. We don't know the extent of the power of that gauntlet."

"What about this?" she asked, holding up the book Honor had given me. "Maybe this has some information?"

"I'm sure it does," I said. "At least, it possesses more information than we currently have, which is nil."

"Not entirely," Tiger said, opening the book. "We know it's a siphon and augmenter. We don't know its range, but I'm pretty sure Fakul wasn't nearby when he sent those puppets after you."

"He alluded to as much," I said. "We also know it can affect targets remotely. The siphon worked on the puppets to make one of them stronger."

"Let me do some research here," she said, holding up the book. "If another way exists, I'll find it."

I nodded.

For all her impetuousness, Tiger possessed a keen mind to solve problems. If there was something in the book that allowed us to use another method besides a void vortex, she would find it.

"In the meantime, we need to procure supplies for Goat," I said. "Specifically, the rune-inscribed tungsten."

"You still want to deceive a dragon?" Tiger asked. "Are you feeing particularly suicidal these days?"

"Char mustn't get her hands on that gauntlet," I said. "Goat assures me he can create a near exact duplicate."

"If anyone can do it, Goat can," Tiger said. "Where are we going to get rune-inscribed tungsten? I doubt Home Depot has a magical materials section."

"We need to go see Heka," I said. "I'll understand if you choose to decline this visit."

"Wordweavers?" Tiger said, glaring at me. "Seriously? Are you trying to make my life miserable?"

"As I said, you're free to decl—"

"And leave you in the Cloisters alone with Aria and her freaks?" Tiger shot back, raising her voice. "Are you insane? I'm coming with."

"I don't think that's such a good idea."

"I didn't ask what you thought," she said with a smile full of malice. "You said I was free to decline. I choose to accept your kind invitation into the Cloisters, thank you."

"If you try to attack them, Aria will incapacitate you," I said, keeping my voice even. "Your kinetic casts are not faster than her words."

"I like Heka."

"It seems you only like Heka," I said. "You understand how quickly Aria can react to any aggressive action on your part? She only needs to whisper a word."

"I'm sure that if I rip her throat out first, she'll have a hard time forming any words, don't you think?"

"We are not mounting an attack on the Wordweavers."

"Pity," Tiger said. "They preach neutrality, but have their hands in everything. I don't like them and I don't trust them."

"You don't need to do either," I said. "Goat and Heka are friends. If we are to procure this material, we need to visit them. Like you said, it will not be easy to locate runed tungsten."

"Don't you have another source?"

"In this time frame? No," I said. "You're going to have to refrain from ripping anyone's throat out while we visit. Can you manage?"

"Not like I have a choice," she grumbled. "My animosity is justified though."

"I never said it wasn't," I replied as we headed uptown, "just that we can't get into a war with the Wordweavers right now. Why don't you pencil it in for a later, more convenient time, when we aren't trying to take down a psychopath who uses mages like disposable dolls?"

"Good point," she said reluctantly. "You know we're going to have to confront them sooner or later."

"Later, much later," I said. "Facing the Wordweavers— Aria especially—will be a significant challenge. It would be mutually beneficial to form a loose alliance of sorts, one that doesn't involve blood or death."

"I make no promises."

I sighed and placed another call. It connected after several seconds.

"Sebastian," the voice said. "this is a pleasant surprise. How can I help you?"

"Hello, Aria," I said, keeping my voice light. "I need to acquire some rare material and wondered if you happened to have some in-house?"

"What kind of material?" Aria asked warily.

Her caution was warranted—not because I was asking, although I would be wary if someone with my reputation was asking for rare magical material. The reason for her wariness had to do more with what an accomplished mage could create with magical material.

By providing me with material, she could inadvertently be supplying me with the components to create some weapon of mass destruction. Needless to say, Wordweavers frowned on that sort of thing.

"I need runed tungsten."

"For? Are you creating armor?"

"Of a sort," I said. "I need enough to create a gauntlet."

"One gauntlet?" she asked. "That sounds impractical. Why only one gauntlet?"

It all hinged on my next comment. If she refused, we would have to obtain the tungsten through illicit means, which would increase the level of danger in this mission exponentially. I had rather not go that route if I could avoid it. As it stood, getting it from Heka was going to incur a heavy cost.

There was always a cost.

I cleared my throat and glanced at Tiger who nodded, while looking positively livid at the turn of events.

"Goat will be replicating the Gauntlet of Mahkah."

Silence.

It went on long enough for me to wonder if we had lost the connection.

"I have it on good authority that the Gauntlets of Mahkah have been destroyed."

"One has, yes," I said. "One is still in play."

"Still in play?" she asked, the wariness replaced with a slight tone of menace. "What exactly do you mean by 'still in play'? Clarify."

I explained the situation with Fakul to her, sticking to the abridged version in an effort to save time.

"Human puppets?" she said, the menace no longer slight. "He used human puppets?"

"Yes, I'm afraid so," I said. "I intend to stop him."

"By stop, you mean kill?"

"Yes," I said. There was nothing to gain by sugarcoating my intentions or lying to her. Besides, she was no delicate flower. Aria had seen her share of battle. "He has shown a willingness to use this gauntlet as a weapon to kill. He must be stopped."

"One moment," she said. "Let me ask Heka if she has what you need."

"Thank you."

The line went quiet, but I refrained from saying anything. Wordweavers were notorious spies, using the power of words against their targets. In their presence, it was best to listen twice as much as you spoke.

She returned to the line, close to a minute later.

"She has the material," Aria said. "But there will be a blood debt."

"Excuse me?" I said. "A blood debt?"

"Bitch," Tiger said under her breath. "Let's get it somewhere else."

"Hello, Tiger," Aria said, the menace in her voice now acquiring a target. "You're welcome to try. You won't find runed tungsten easily obtainable."

"Why not?" I asked, genuinely curious.

"Those who do have it won't part with it, and those who will part with what they have will offer you an alloy, not pure runed tungsten," she said. "The choice is yours. If you intend on making a copy of the gauntlet, I can only assume it's to use it as some kind of decoy. For that you need pure runed tungsten."

Aria was always able to see several steps ahead of those who faced her. She didn't become the leader of the Word-weavers on this continent by being naive and gullible.

"What is the blood debt?" Tiger asked. "What does Heka want?"

"Nothing from you," Aria replied dryly. "Sebastian would have to pay the blood debt."

"Sebastian, not Goat?"

"Goat isn't the one making the request," Aria said. "Sebastian will have to pay the blood debt. I assume you're headed here?"

"We are," I said, knowing full well that she knew we were on our way. She was just being courteous. "What is the blood debt?"

"It has several parts," Aria said. "Heka has to be part of the process, she was very specific about that."

"I doubt Goat would travel to the Cloisters," I said. "He prefers to remain indoors."

"One moment."

Silence again. I glanced at the now seething Tiger beside me. We had crossed the city and were currently heading uptown on the Henry Hudson Parkway. The Cloisters, the Wordweaver base of operations, was located near the northernmost tip of the city, atop a tall hill in Fort Tryon Park.

Stepping into the Cloisters was similar to stepping back in time. All of the architecture was medieval, a combination of several ancient monasteries joined to create one immense nexus of power—controlled by the Wordweavers.

I gestured and created a sphere of silence inside the Tank.

"A blood debt, really?" Tiger asked as we sped uptown. "What are our options?"

"I'm afraid Aria's right," I said, maneuvering around traffic. "If this material is so rare that it requires a blood debt, trying to find it elsewhere will prove to be difficult, if not impossible."

"What about SuNaTran?" Tiger asked, tapping the interior of the Tank. "Cecil works with metals, maybe he has some?"

"I doubt it," I said. "Tungsten is strong, and I'm sure runed tungsten is stronger still, but from my understanding, it's brittle. Reinforcing vehicles with metal that could shatter on impact is bound to have a negative effect on SuNaTran's reputation for safe vehicles."

"True, that would suck," Tiger agreed. "Why the blood debt though?"

Aria came back on the line and I disabled the sphere of silence.

"Heka will arrange to travel to your headquarters as soon as the blood debt is paid," Aria said. "Do you agree to the payment of the blood debt?"

"Sight unseen?" I asked. "You haven't shared what the actual cost will be."

"I know. You still have a choice."

"What choice?" Tiger demanded. "Either he agrees, or he doesn't get the metal. What kind of choice is that?"

"An informed one," Aria said, her reply curt. "What shall it be, Sebastian?"

"We'll be there in ten minutes."

"I will take that as a yes, and make the appropriate preparations."

"Please do," I said, glancing at Tiger. "Thank you."

"I doubt you will want to thank me after you learn the cost," Aria said. "I will see you soon."

TWENTY-TWO

"You can't do this," Tiger protested. "A blood debt is bad, but one to Wordweavers? That's...that's ten times worse."

"Only ten times?"

"This isn't funny," Tiger said, her voice grim. "Not even remotely. A Wordweaver blood cost could be anything. You could end up being a slave to Aria and her freaks."

"I have no intention of being anyone's slave," I said, matching the intensity in her voice. "If the cost is too high, I will refuse."

"Bullshit," she spat. "You want to stop Fakul—"

"Don't you?"

"I'd like to punch my fist into his intestines and slowly eviscerate the fucker," she said. "But I'm not willing to give up my life for it."

"Nor am I," I said. "Thank you for that visual by the way, but I'm not giving—"

"Save it," she said, resigned to the fact that this was happening. "For someone who keeps saying they aren't a hero, you sure enjoy acting like one most of the time."

"Fakul needs to be stopped," I said. "Char can't get that gauntlet. It's that simple and that complicated."

"Why does that have to include you entering into a blood debt with the Wordweavers?"

"I'm open to suggestions if you have an alternate method of getting the runed tungsten?" I said. "Any come to mind?"

"No," she said with a low growl. "You know I don't."

"Then this is the best and fastest way to get what we need, agreed?"

"I'm not agreeing to anything," she said. "You may be doing this, but I'm not in agreement. At all."

"I will take your vote of no confidence into consideration," I said, ending the discussion. "Follow up with Rat and see how much progress he's made on the information I sent you."

She pulled out her phone and dialed the Directive.

Her conversation with Rabbit was brief before she was rerouted to Rat. That conversation was terse, and I was certain Rat sensed she was upset. In the end, he opted for sending us the information instead of discussing the details with Tiger.

No one enjoyed speaking with Tiger when she was upset.

"He's sending over the information," she said. "Should be downloading now."

I pressed the display on the Tank and saw the file arrive. With the touch of a few buttons, the file was also sent to my and Tiger's phones. A few minutes later, we arrived at the main entrance to the Cloisters.

Aria stood outside in the midday sun, wearing a black T-shirt and blue jeans. The shirt, which was covered in white stylized lettering, read: *We set our expectations low...so you can meet them. -The Dive.*

Her long, black hair was loose and she brushed a few

strands out of her face as she gazed at us. Tiger and I left the Tank and approached the main entrance.

I noticed that the runes around the entrance and throughout the property pulsed with violet and golden power. The energy being emitted by the failsafes was considerable.

"Well met," she said as we closed the distance. "Heka will be with us shortly."

I gazed down at her shirt and smiled despite myself.

"The Dive?" I asked. "Is that an actual place?"

She glanced down at her shirt.

"Actually, yes," she said. "Though I don't think it's your kind of establishment." She gave Tiger a look. "It's more her kind of place."

"My kind of place?" Tiger said. "What's that supposed to mean?"

"The Dive is Grey Stryder's place of business and residence. It serves as a de facto and unofficial neutral zone."

"The Night Warden?" I asked. "I wasn't aware he had *two* locations in the city. I am familiar with the Abyss."

"How does that make it my kind of place?" Tiger asked as her anger nudged into dangerous territory. "What are you trying to say?"

Aria was unfazed and continued.

"Though it has been recognized by the Councils and every pertinent authority as a neutral zone, it has been exploded, attacked, and surveilled, along with numerous attempts on Grey's life occurring within the premises."

"What kind of neutral zone is that?" I asked. "It sounds more dangerous inside than out."

"Which is why I said it's more her kind of place," Aria answered, glancing at Tiger. "It's a place where you go to disappear and be left alone, not a place to be seen."

"Actually," Tiger said with a mischievous smile, "that does sound like my kind of place."

"I thought so," Aria said. "Please come inside."

She turned and headed inside.

We stood in one of the ornately designed foyers. Sofas and chairs were situated around the room for guests visiting the Cloisters. Part of the property still functioned as an arm for the Met Museum and regularly allowed guests to visit.

How that worked with the constant threat by enemies was a mystery to me. The area we stood in was an informal space, not open to the general public, designed for visiting mages to consult with the Wordweavers on daily magical business.

This particular foyer was designed like the hub of a wheel, with several passages leading away from it like the spokes. Each passageway was accessed by one of the identical doors around the room.

Beyond the doors the passageways led to the official meeting rooms; these were secured with specific runes to prevent and curtail any type of eavesdropping.

Tiger and I both knew better than to attempt any of the doors without Aria. The Wordweavers were famous—and in some circles infamous—for their Corridors of Chaos. Beyond each of the doors, was a magical labyrinth designed to trap anyone unfortunate enough to venture into the passages.

Entering the Corridors without a Wordweaver, a person would wander around hopelessly lost, until they were rescued or died from exposure—exposure to the lethal failsafes that made up the defenses of the Corridors.

The Wordweavers weren't known for their compassion or mercy.

"This way, please," Aria said as she opened a door. "Heka is waiting for us in her Armory."

"I hate these damn corridors," Tiger grumbled under her breath. "Can't Heka just meet us here?"

"I'm afraid not," Aria said, holding the door open with a slight smile across her lips. "This is a necessary precaution."

"Necessary precaution my ass," Tiger snapped. "You know I hate these passages. You're doing this on purpose."

"I have no idea what you're talking about," Aria said, feigning innocence. "Are you implying that I would *deliberately* subject you to the Corridors of Chaos?"

"That's exactly what I'm saying, there's no implying," Tiger shot back. "You're doing this on purpose because you get some sadistic thrill from it."

"I can assure you," Aria said, her voice low and cold, "had I wanted to torture you, I would have devised something more appropriate for you. Perhaps something along the lines of a few weeks in a sensory deprivation cell? I think that would be enough to push you over the edge. Wouldn't you agree?"

"You wouldn't," Tiger said, her voice a not-so-veiled threat. She glared at Aria as she came to a stop before the door. She turned to face me. "If she did, I'm staying right here."

I gave Aria a pointed look.

"You're right," Aria said, returning my look. "I wouldn't, but if I ever needed to deter you from violence...there are ways."

"This is why I didn't want to come here," Tiger said, step-ping past the door. "She's loving this. Her face doesn't show it, but inside, I know she does."

I shook my head and sighed.

I stepped past the threshold as Aria closed the door behind us. The entire corridor shifted, and I could feel the sensation of horizontal motion; a few seconds later, it angled slightly downward.

At the end of the corridor, in the dim light I could just

barely make out a door. The door at the end of the corridor looked out of place. It appeared to be a large vault door.

"Is this door designed to protect what's behind it, or is it designed to keep whatever is inside in?" I asked. "It looks formidable."

"It is," Aria said with a glance at the door. "It's designed to be a bit of both. Heka occasionally works with unstable runes. In most cases, this door is designed to keep whatever she unleashes from destroying the rest of the Cloisters."

"She's almost as bad as Goat," I said. "His workshop is off-limits to most of us."

"Only if we want to stay alive," Tiger said. "Goat is certifiable."

"I'd say they were both cut from the same cloth," Aria added. "An insatiable curiosity and the fearlessness to pursue where it may lead."

Aria looked at me, then her gaze lowered to the pendant that hung around my neck.

"Where did you get that?" she continued. "I haven't seen a vortex isolator of that caliber in many years. Are you planning on unleashing armageddon anytime soon?"

"Hopefully not," I said, touching the isolator with a hand. "This is something I need in order to deal with Fakul."

"Deal with Fakul?" she asked pensively. "Does that include unleashing a vortex to be held by that isolator?"

"Yes."

"I really hope it doesn't come to that," Aria said, still focused on the isolator. "Heka will want to look at that. It's possible she has another method for you, one that doesn't require its use."

As I had said, Aria was incredibly perceptive.

She knew that the only reason I would be wearing a vortex isolator of this kind was if I planned on unleashing a cast powerful enough to destroy me and most of the tri-state —if I let it get out of control.

"She's welcome to examine it," I said. "But I don't think she can improve on it. I've never seen one like it."

"Nor have I," Aria agreed. "But she is adept at modifying and enhancing artifacts."

"So where is she?" Tiger asked. "Are we supposed to stand here all day?"

"She will be here shortly," Aria said, glancing at the vault door. "She is suspending the test to allow you entry."

"Suspending the test? What test?"

"The one that would gain you entry to the Armory had you been here under different circumstances."

"Out of curiosity, what exactly is this test?"

"Nothing too extreme," Aria said. "It would depend on what she was testing for on any particular day. With you two"—she gave us the once-over—"she would probably use obliteration orbs, some illusions to test your sight ability, and something to counter Tiger's mastery of kinetic casts."

Tiger glared at me. The look said: *I told you they were a bunch of sadistic freaks.*

"But she's not using the test, correct?" I asked to make sure we weren't about to be attacked. "It's being completely disabled?"

"Yes, because of the blood debt," Aria said. "She was planning on reaching out to Grey, but you actually make a better candidate."

"I do? Why?"

"Grey is a complicated individual," Aria said. "There are many things he is capable of, but there are some, well, there are some things he won't do. Things that would require violence."

"You're saying Grey is a peaceful Night Warden all of sudden?"

Tiger laughed at that.

"Are we talking about the same Night Warden?" she asked between laughs. "The one bonded to a murderous sword. *That* peaceful Night Warden?"

"As I said, he is a complicated individual," Aria said. "He has certain...principles he will not violate. Even if it means losing his life."

"Are you calling me unprincipled?"

"You are pragmatic," she said. "You are capable and willing to do what needs to be done."

"Sounds like she's calling you unprincipled," Tiger said with a chuckle. "I mean she's not wrong, but it's still a back-handed compliment."

"Should I be concerned about the nature of this blood debt?"

The vault door slid open into a recessed slot in the wall. Upon further examination, I realized that breaching the armory would be close to impossible. Orange runes came to life on the floor, the surrounding walls, and the door itself, as it slid open.

"Come in, please," Heka said from inside. "I'll explain everything."

TWENTY-THREE

I had met Heka several times in the past.

Each time I saw her, the impression she made was one of immeasurable power, both physical and magical. Her energy signature read a close second to Aria. She was quite large, built like a powerlifter who spent copious hours in a temple of iron, lifting astounding weights in the pursuit of strength, power, and girth.

She wore a thick, heavyweight, full grain leather apron, covered in runes. The apron extended from her shoulders to just above her knees.

Her black hair was pulled back and kept under a golden, runed-covered bandana. She had a genuine smile on her face and opened her arms to hug Tiger who wholeheartedly returned the hug.

There were few people on this planct that Tiger hugged, at least without driving a blade into their abdomen afterwards. Heka was one of the few who not only could get physically close to Tiger, but also enjoyed the demonstration of affection from her.

"How is Goat?" Heka asked as a flicker of violet energy shimmered across her eyes. "Is he still blowing things up?"

"You know Goat," Tiger said with a smile. "He won't leave his cave, and he's still up to his projects. He's working on some claws for me."

"Claws?" I said as Heka laughed. "You never mentioned anything about claws. Why would he make you claws?"

"Hello?" Tiger said, giving me a look. "My name is Tiger, and every tiger should have claws." She turned to Heka. "Don't you agree?"

"Why do you need claws?" I protested. "Are you saying you're not lethal enough?"

"That sounds like a great idea," she said. "I'll ask him about this latest claw project when I see him. Maybe we can make them even more lethal."

"More lethal? That sounds like a horrendous idea," I said, rubbing my face. "Why would you want to do that?"

"Claws are not friendly weapons," Heka said. "Everyone knows this—you especially should know this, Sebastian, but they can be quite useful in making a point."

"What does that mean?" I asked, suddenly offended. "I don't have claws of any sort."

Heka raised an eyebrow and gave me an incredulous look.

"Your karambits seem to be very claw-like to me," Heka said. "Close quarter blades designed to rip, hook, and shred. Those sound like claws to me."

"Me too," Tiger said. "Wouldn't you agree, Sebastian?"

I remained silent, not because I lacked an answer. I had plenty, but all of them would only make this delicate situation considerably worse.

Also, I remained silent because they were right. My karambits had been named the Dragon's Claws by more than one enemy unfortunate enough to face me.

"Be that as it may," I said, waving Tiger's words away. "If

you would be so kind, Heka, this blood debt. Explain it to me."

"It's simple really," she said, her expression darkening. "I was working with a sacred amethyst; it was stolen by someone I trusted. I need it back."

It couldn't have been *that* simple.

"That sounds simple enough," I said, staring at her. "Why not give me the complicated details?"

"The thief was a Sister," Heka began, "my apprentice. Someone I trusted."

"That we apprehended and retired," Aria added. "She will never steal from the Wordweavers again."

"Or anyone else, I would imagine," I said. "And this sacred amethyst?"

"She had delivered it before we caught her," Heka said, glancing at Aria who looked away. In typical Word-weaver fashion, there was much more going on here than they were explaining. "We moved too slowly to stop the trade."

"Trade? Who did she trade it to, and what for?"

"She traded it to Maledicta for the promise of power, prestige, and money."

"I thought the Sisters relinquished all attachments to the material world when they joined the order," I said. "How did this happen?"

"We are powerful, not perfect," Aria said with a trace of frustration in her voice. "Even we can succumb to tempta-tion, as Amina did."

"I see," I said, not really seeing. "Who or what is Maledicta?"

"Maledicta is a group of assassins," Heka clarified. "Very few know of their existence, within or outside the magical community."

"They're certainly doing a good job of keeping a low

profile," I said with a nod. "This is the first time I've heard of them."

"That's not surprising," Heka said. "There's more."

"There always is," I said. "Please continue."

"They're not just assassins," she said, looking tentatively at Aria who nodded. "They're also dark mages."

I sighed. This was going to be more complicated than I imagined.

"Holy hell," Tiger said. "You want us to go up against mage assassins for a jewel?"

"Not just *any* jewel," Heka said and then hesitated. "I was imbuing this jewel with special properties."

"May as well give us the full picture," I said. "What does this jewel do? How did you modify it?"

"This was all experimental," Heka said. "I didn't think it would actually work."

"Apparently one of your Sisters believed it would—enough to betray you and risk her life to steal from the Word-weavers," I said. "What properties did you imbue the jewel with?"

"It's a corrupted amplifier," Heka said, her voice low. "Something like a last resort one-time use weapon. I was testing out the properties to see if they could be imbued in other items, actual weapons. The jewel was a safe conduit due to its configuration. I don't think it works, but if it does, we are in serious trouble."

That much I understood.

Throughout history, jewels had been used to hold vast amounts of power or special casts because their structure created a stable container of sorts. They were excellent for testing out dangerous casts without running the risk of reducing yourself to atoms in the process.

"Would you mind clarifying what a corrupted amplifier does?"

"It takes a powerful mage and shifts them," Heka said. "It's a major shift."

I didn't like the sound of that.

"How major of a shift?" Tiger asked. "How far does it shift them?"

"I don't know," Heka admitted. "I was conducting tests and theories when Amina stole it."

"If you had to guess," I said, "how far could it shift a mage?"

"There are so many variables: it depends on their current power level, how far they're willing to assimilate the amethyst—"

"How far they're willing to what?"

"In order for the properties to manifest, the sacred amethyst must be assimilated," she said. "The mage in question would have to be exceptionally powerful to be able to do that."

"You mean take it into their body? Merge with it?"

"If they're strong enough yes. If not, they would have to wear it," she said. "The effects wouldn't be as pronounced, but it would still enhance the mage's ability."

"Hypothetically speaking, let's say a mage is able to completely assimilate it, what then?"

"According to my theories, they would shift and most likely die as a result," Heka answered. "But if they survived the shift—"

"Yes?"

"You'd be looking at someone near Archmage level— instantly," she said. "That's why I called it the sacred amethyst. It could turn a mage into nearly a god."

"If they were powerful enough and survived the assimilation," I said, rolling this problem over in my head. "Does someone like this exist in this Maledicta group?"

"Not currently, no," Aria said. "That's not our main concern."

"You think they may try to sell it," Tiger said. "To someone who *is* strong enough."

Aria nodded.

"Tell me about the other part of this amplifier, the corrupted part."

Heka sighed and looked away.

"Tell him," Aria said. "He deserves to know it all, if you want his blood debt."

"The sacred amethyst has a lethal failsafe," Heka said. "At first, I thought it was an anomaly, but with each iteration the same side effect would appear, so I incorporated the side effect into a failsafe."

"What side effect?"

"If a mage manages to successfully assimilate it, they have about a month before the process is irreversible," Heka said. "After that, another month on the outside."

"Another month of what?"

"Of life," Heka added. "It corrupts the mage, devouring the mind and body. They will be powerful, but slowly go insane, before the sacred amethyst collapses. It seems the power influx destabilizes the jewel."

"And the mage in question."

"True, after a month it reaches its limit," she said. "Then it implodes."

"And you haven't managed to find a way to stabilize the jewel in question?"

"I've tried every jewel known to hold a cast; amethyst held it the longest," she answered. "The result was the same. They all collapse after a certain amount of time."

"What possessed you to create such a thing?" Tiger asked, the anger thick in her voice. "Please tell me you know where this magical time bomb is."

"Yes," Aria answered. "We have Maledicta under surveillance."

"So why not just go in and get the amethyst back?" Tiger said. "Go in, words blazing, and shred them."

"We tried that," Aria said. "We retrieved the bodies of several of our sisters with their throats cut. An effective way to silence a Wordweaver."

Tiger gave me a dark look.

"This Amina told them," Tiger said. "Did you leave her alive?"

"We did, for now," Aria said. "She has information we need. We have been able to extract most of it, but—"

"You don't have someone who can act on it," I said. "They know how to effectively counter a Wordweaver."

"We are Wordweavers, not assassins," Aria answered. "We cannot meet them on their battlefield."

"You need to rectify that, stat," Tiger said. "Start a Word-weaver Special Ops group; call them Nightweavers or some-thing. Seriously. You are unprepared for this threat."

"Exactly; that's why we need the blood debt," Heka said, staring at me. "It's not just *your* blood debt."

"What do you mean?" I asked. "Who else—?"

Heka reached into her apron and produced a large, black, rune-covered blade. Its energy signature was hidden, until she drew it out into the open. Now that she held it in her hand, an oppressive energy emanated from it.

"I caused this and I will resolve it, even if it means I must sacrifice my life in the process, this I swear," she said, slicing her hand, before handing me the blade, hilt first. It pulsed with power as it absorbed the blood from her hand. "Do you accept this blood debt?"

I looked down at the blade. Though I didn't adhere to the tenets of the Wordweavers, I was close to Aria. We were friends and I had too few of those in my life. That being said,

I couldn't in good conscience drag the entire Directive into a battle with mage assassins.

"This blood debt only applies to me, correct?" I asked clarifying the conditions. "No one else will be forced to comply to the conditions?"

"That is how blood debts work," Heka said. "This will only apply to us two."

"There is no way I'm letting you face mage assassins alone," Tiger said under her breath. "If you do this, know that all of the Directive will be involved."

I nodded.

"But only *I* would suffer the consequences of a broken blood debt," I said. "The rest of the Directive would be free of the contract."

"That changes nothing," Tiger said. "You are not doing this alone."

I turned to Heka.

"I will help you retrieve the sacred amethyst, even if it means sacrificing my life," I said. "Once retrieved, you *will* destroy this jewel. This I swear."

I ran the blade across my palm and clasped Heka's wounded hand. The blade absorbed my blood. A wave of energy rippled out from both Heka and me. If we violated this blood debt, it would be better to end our lives in the most horrific manner conceivable, than to withstand the consequences of a broken blood debt.

Tiger looked on with an expression of resigned finality.

"How soon before this Maledicta moves with the amethyst?" Tiger asked. "I only ask because we still have a psychomage puppeteer roaming the streets that we need to stop."

"Since they don't have someone strong enough among their ranks," Aria said, "they have reached out to other, less than reputable groups for buyers. So far, nothing."

"Fine, we're on a timetable," I said. "Aria, I trust you will keep monitoring the Maledicta situation, and notify us if anything changes. In the meantime, we have a gauntlet to fake, a dragon to deceive, and a puppeteer to stop...permanently."

"Right," Heka said, gazing at my chest. "Before I go, can I examine that vortex isolator a little closer?"

I removed the chain and handed the pendant to Heka.

"You want to be careful with that," I said. "It's supposed to be able to hold a void vortex."

"It will," she said. "For about ten minutes, before it explodes in your face and destroys everything around you."

"When you say 'destroys everything', you mean—?"

"Everything. You, the ground you stand on, the city you're currently inhabiting, and maybe some of the adjoining states."

"That would be less than ideal."

"Where did you get this?" Heka asked. "It's not inferior quality, but the holding capacity can be increased."

"Ivory," I said.

"Ivory?" Heka asked examining the pendant. "That makes sense. She can access powerful artifacts, but she can't shape them. I'm surprised she gave this to you. It's quite rare to find a vortex isolator this powerful."

"I asked nicely," I said. "Can you improve it? Ten minutes doesn't sound nearly long enough."

"I can increase the delay," she said, turning it over in her hand. "Buy you some more time, but the end result will be the same. It's not meant to hold a vortex indefinitely, I don't think anything can."

"How long?"

"I can increase the delay to an hour," she said with a confident nod. "After that, you need to power down the vortex, if you can, or toss this pendant into a void space."

"That would work, thank you," I said. "How long until you're ready to head to Goat?"

"This will take half an hour, then I'll take the materials to Goat," she said. "After that, I need to see the schematics of the gauntlet before I can give you a time of completion, but with both of us working on it, I don't see it taking more than a day or two. The hardest part of creating a gauntlet like that is the runework and getting the tungsten."

"Fair enough," I said. "I'll have Goat get ready for you."

"In the meantime, we need to have a word, Sebastian," Aria said. "Please come with me, both of you."

She headed to the large vault door.

I looked at Tiger who shrugged, motioning for me to go first. She turned to Heka and nodded, before giving her a hug and catching up to me.

TWENTY-FOUR

After several minutes and countless turns, assuring we were completely lost, we arrived in a spacious sitting room which also doubled as a library of sorts.

"Please sit," Aria said, motioning to one of the comfortable wingback chairs situated around the small, round tables. She sat down and leaned back letting out a small sigh. "That is pleasant."

I kept looking around the room, admiring the coziness of the space. When I took a seat, a sense of contentment came over me. That's when I noticed the runes woven into the chairs.

"You've created a room of solace," I said, enjoying the sensation of comfort. "I've been meaning to create one for the Directive, but haven't made the time."

"I find it to be an essential part of my day, even if only for a few minutes," she said. "It helps keep me sane."

"This is nice," Tiger said. "We definitely need one of these at the Church."

I nodded.

"You wanted to speak to us?" I asked. "About?"

"I understand the course of action you are taking," she said. "Destroying the gauntlet is the right choice."

"It's the only choice," I said. "Giving it to Char would be an error with far-reaching implications."

"That is what I wanted to discuss with you," she said, her voice grim. "Are you certain it's wise to deceive her? If she handles it poorly, you will have made a formidable enemy."

I sat back for a moment and steepled my hands as I gazed off into the distance.

"If I give her the gauntlet, any further damage it causes will be my responsibility," I said. "I won't accept that, not while I can remove it from play."

"If she declares war on the Directive, she will also declare war on the Wordweavers," Aria added, keeping her voice low. "Have you considered this?"

"Why would she declare war on the Wordweavers?" Tiger asked. "Sebastian is the one who is fooling her."

"By assisting you in this ruse, our futures are intertwined," Aria said. "If she seeks retribution for this slight, she will retaliate against all parties involved."

"That won't happen," I said, my voice firm. "Char is... powerful, yes. I can, however, dissuade her from taking any action against the Wordweavers and the Directive."

Aria stared at me for a few seconds before nodding.

"I will trust your judgement in this," she said. After a few more moments of silence, "I also wanted to express my thanks. I had no wish to sacrifice more sisters in the retrieval of the sacred amethyst."

"So you're willing to sacrifice Sebastian?" Tiger asked. "That's nice."

"As you said, my sisters are not prepared for this kind of warfare," Aria said, turning to Tiger. "Perhaps, when you have some time, you can help form a group of...Nightweavers."

"Are you serious?" Tiger said, narrowing her eyes at Aria. "This isn't some kind of joke?"

"I've realized the necessity for a special combat unit within the sisters for some time now," Aria replied, looking off to the side into some recent memory, "especially after dealing repeatedly with Tristan and Simon. It's come to my attention how ill-equipped we are at dealing with high-level threats."

"Those two are a high-level threat all on their own," Tiger said. "Fine, I'll do it on one condition."

"Which is?"

"Clothing," Tiger said, causing me to raise an eyebrow. "A full ensemble for me and the Directive."

"The entire Directive?" Aria asked with a small smile. "That is no small task."

"Tiger..." I began before she shot me a look that derailed my train of thought.

"She wants a special ops team," Tiger said, looking at Aria. "I can do that, but I'm going to need Wordweaver clothing."

"But the whole Directive?"

"Fine, I'll compromise," Tiger said. "All of the members of the Directive that engage in field work."

I nodded.

That was about half of us, which was still an astounding amount of rune-enhanced Wordweaver clothing.

"Which is about half the Directive, if I'm not mistaken?" Aria said. "Very well, that I can agree to."

"Start with him. He was busy getting himself bounced around this morning," Tiger said, pointing at me. "Zegna and Armani are pretty, but they were doing squat for you, as you imitated a piñata today. You need function over looks."

I looked down at my suit.

"My clothing is more than adequate, thank you."

"We do have some suits from the House of Zegna that we

have enhanced," Aria said. "I'll make sure you leave with them, once Heka is done with your vortex isolator."

"Thank you," I said as Tiger's phone vibrated. She excused herself, stood and walked away to take the call. "Have you ever dealt with puppeteers?"

"I'm afraid not," Aria said. "None of the Sisters under my tenure have exhibited that particular skill. From my understanding, it's quite rare."

"Fakul, with this gauntlet, poses a considerable threat," I said. "I've never run across anything like it. These mages were willing to sacrifice their lives for him."

"If what you described is accurate, it seems to operate on the subjugation of will," Aria said, "very similar to a state of zealotry. In order for that state to exist, the will of the subjects must be weak to begin with."

"Creating a fertile ground for the gauntlet to work?"

"That is not entirely the work of the gauntlet, at least not at first," Aria said. "It's possible this Fakul is a charismatic individual who entices those who crave power or lack an identity, to join his cause."

"His cause?"

"Individuals who engage in this behavior usually have a driving cause, something that spurs them on," Aria said. "What is Fakul's cause?"

"I don't know," I said pensively. "There was plenty of 'ushering in a new age', and his willingness to sacrifice his human puppets demonstrated an acute disdain for the value of life."

"Some revel in power for power's sake."

"And some just want to watch the world burn while pouring gasoline on the flames," I said. "I truly think he is mad."

"Do not confuse madness for simple evil," she said. "He may be mad, but he possesses power."

"Then that power is magnifying this evil."

She nodded.

"If you want to defeat him, it would be best to discover what truly drives him, and undermine it," she said. "If you can sow doubt in his subjects, you can weaken his hold on them. Otherwise you will face an army of human mage puppets bent on your destruction."

"That is not a situation I look forward to—"

The door to the sitting room opened, and Heka stepped in just as Tiger ended her call.

"I was able to get it done a little faster," Heka said, handing me the chain and pendant. "This really is a fascinating artifact. If you speak to Ivory again, I would be interested in learning where she found it."

"I will let her know you're interested in its origins," I said, placing the chain and pendant around my neck. "Are you headed over to Goat now?"

"Yes," Heka said, looking at Aria. "The Armory is closed, but you have the access runes. I don't anticipate being gone more than a few days, but I should get going now."

"Same applies to us," Tiger said, putting her phone away. "That was Rat. We need to go—now."

Aria nodded and gestured.

"Your suits are in your vehicle," Aria said. "I do hope they serve you well."

"Thank you, again," I said. "If it all goes according to plan, I will only have to worry about an upset dragon."

"An upset dragon?" Tiger said. "That's all? And here I was, worried."

"We will stand with you if need be, Sebastian," Aria said. "I wish you the best fortune in this endeavor."

"Thank you," I said. "We'll speak soon."

"Remember my words: find the seed of doubt and plant

it," Aria said. "Heka, if you would be so kind as to lead our guests out?"

"Of course," Heka said. "This way."

Aria remained seated and watched us leave.

TWENTY-FIVE

Heka led us out of the sitting room and down the dimly lit Corridors of Chaos. Every so often, she would stop at an intersection and read the small plaques on the walls.

I also noticed that some of the walls had hidden runes inscribed beneath some of the plaques, with explicit instructions on where to turn or which corridor to avoid.

I made no mention of the hidden runes for several reasons. I wasn't supposed to be able to see them, which meant that my ability had come into play. Revealing that I could see them meant losing an advantage no one knew I had. Also, something else was at work here, besides my abilities. I could read these runes, even though they had been written in proto-runes, which were normally illegible to me.

"You sure you know where you're going?" Tiger asked after our next turn at an intersection. "Because it feels like you're lost."

"I may be the chief runesmith, but I'm a Sister of the order," Heka said, walking forward confidently. "Part of my duties as runesmith is to be able to navigate the Corridors of

Chaos. If I couldn't, Aria wouldn't have asked me to lead you out."

"I'm just asking because you and Goat are similar—he never leaves his workshop," Tiger said. "I figured you didn't get much practice wandering these corridors either and I noticed you reading the plaques."

"Better safe than sorry," Heka said with a smile. "It's true, I don't wander the corridors much, but I don't get lost—ever. I'll get you to the entrance, then make my way to Goat."

"That actually works out," Tiger said, giving me a look. "We need to go look at a location."

"We do?" I asked. "What location?"

"The one that Rat just shared with me," Tiger answered, as I deciphered her look of: *We can't take Heka with us for this*. "That one."

"Right, that one," I said. "Thank you for leading us out, Heka."

"My pleasure," she said, oblivious to the silent exchange between Tiger and me. "I'll have Goat contact you once we get an idea of how much time it's going to take to duplicate your gauntlet."

"I would appreciate that, thank you," I said as we reached the main entrance. "I have a feeling time is of the essence. Goat will explain the details of the project."

"I'm sure he will," she said, squeezing Tiger's shoulder and leaning in. "Try not to get into too much trouble. If your claws are ready, I'll enhance them and send them over first."

"Give them to Rat, he can get them to me the fastest." Tiger said, lowering her voice. "For the record, I never get into trouble,"

"True, you're usually the trouble itself," Heka said. "I'll see you at the Church, if you get back before I'm done."

Tiger nodded as Heka walked away.

We stepped outside and approached the Tank. I placed

my hand on its surface, unlocking it with a flash of orange energy. Sitting in the back seat were several black suits.

"Aria bypassed the runes in the Tank?" Tiger asked, pointing at the suits. "How?"

"She's strong enough," I said, gazing at the garments in the back seat. "Something to consider when you insist on confronting her."

The runework in the fabric indicated that they were considerably stronger than the suit I was currently wearing. If I looked carefully, I could see the violet runes pulse slowly.

"She wasn't joking when she said enhanced," Tiger said, looking at the suits. "Those should prevent you from becoming a punching bag if we encounter any more of Fakul's puppets."

"They are quite impressive," I said. "What did Rat say?"

"Check your phone," Tiger said. "He confirmed the Jane Doe. She really was one of Honor's agents."

I accessed the file on my phone and read the information.

"She was a mid-level mage and had managed to infiltrate Umbra," I said. "Her cover was blown because of something called the Rite of Loyalty. Did Rat elaborate on what this rite is?"

"Just that it has something to do with the gauntlet," Tiger said. "Read the next part, the part about where Rat thinks they're headquartered."

I continued reading the file, and a cold dread filled me as I read what Rat had relayed to us according to his investigation of Umbra's area of operations.

"This isn't where I saw Umbra's people," I said. "How sure is he of this information?"

"It's Rat," Tiger said. "He wouldn't have sent it over if he didn't think it was accurate; you know how he is."

She was right.

Rat was beyond meticulous when it came to his information gathering.

"This presents a major problem," I said, rereading the file. "According to Rat, Umbra is operating out of the Hybrid."

"Makes sense," she said as I started the engine. "The Hybrid is a sovereign enclave. None of the Councils can touch it, and the NYTF wouldn't dream of stepping in there."

"It also explains the ELP designation on Honor's agent," I said. "They've been notorious for disappearing people in the past."

"Not even Char would interfere with the Hybrid," Tiger said. "And she's been known to interfere with everyone."

"True, but the group I saw uptown weren't Hybrid clientele," I said. "Those were lower echelon mages."

"You met the grunts," she said, strapping in. "The leadership of Umbra wasn't in ronin territory. They would be somewhere they couldn't be touched."

"You think all of the leadership is in the Hybrid?" I said. "I find that unlikely."

"Maybe not all of the leadership. If Fakul is smart, he would have them spread out, but I'm willing to bet at least Fakul is enjoying the comfort of the Hybrid," Tiger said. "He may be using the club as cover—Castor and Pollux are fringe as it is. Extending the protection of the club to Fakul sounds like something they would do, especially Pollux."

"We don't have an army to storm the Hybrid," I said. "Not that I would want to, even if we did."

"We don't need to storm the Hybrid," Tiger said. "If Fakul is in there, we need the Hybrid to look the other way while we retire him."

"We'd have to force them to rescind their protection, if he is there," I said, "which is easier said than done. The Hybrid is known for its ironclad policy of protection. It's part of what makes them a sanctuary for those avoiding the authorities."

"They may be a sovereign enclave, but they still have to operate in this city," Tiger said. "We're going to have to convince them that it's in their best interests to remove their protection from Fakul."

"How do you propose we do that?"

"What if the Hybrid were to become unsafe for its guests?" she said. "They value their reputation above everything else, don't they?"

"It's one of the most important things they have—their reputation. Damage or threaten that, and it would force them to act."

"Then we know what we need to do," she said with a cold smile. "We press them where it hurts, until they give us Fakul."

"They're going to resist," I said.

"Then we press them harder," she said, "until they give him up."

"I need to speak to Castor first," I said. "Give him an opportunity to do this with minimal damage."

"Good chance he won't listen. I can guarantee Pollux won't listen," she said as we sped downtown. "They'll dismiss your request."

"I'll be nice until it's time not to be nice," I said. "Get Ox on the line."

She called him and rerouted the call through the Tank.

"What's new, Boss?"

"We're paying the Hybrid a visit," I said. "Rat thinks our target is enjoying the comfort and protection of the club."

"If Rat says the target is there, the target is there," Ox said. "What do you need me to do? I'd have to outsource a force large enough to breach the Hybrid."

"No breaching required," I said. "We just need to

convince the management that protecting this specific client would be bad for business."

"Castor and Pollux won't be happy about this," Ox said. "They will seek some kind of retribution, and I like the Church being intact. We already had one headquarters exploded."

"I need you to bring something that sounds dangerous, but causes little to no damage," I said. "We're not going to destroy the Hybrid, we're going after something a little more delicate."

"More delicate?"

"Their reputation of safety," I said. "I want the guests to feel unsafe."

"I see," Ox said, his voice pensive. "You want Castor and Pollux—especially Pollux—to kill you."

"I'll deal with Pollux," I said. "If the Hybrid feels unsafe, they will be willing to give up the target, rather than lose the rest of their clientele and, more importantly, their stellar reputation of protection."

"What time are you looking for this to happen?"

"A little past sunset tonight," I said. "We're heading over there now to have a conversation. If we can't resolve this amicably, well, then we'll have to resort to violence."

"Speaking of violence," Ox said, "where's Tiger?"

"Right here," she said. "What?"

"No, nothing," Ox said quickly. "Just figured you'd be at ground zero for this plan."

"Damn straight," she said. "Bring some RPGs too."

"RPGs are not low damage," Ox said. "Boss said 'sounds dangerous'. Are we looking for a body count here?"

"No, we are not," I said, glancing at Tiger. "We're not trying to kill the guests, just scare them."

"You'd better tell her that," Ox said. "I'll pack low impact, high volume munitions. I'll be there a little after sunset. I'll start the show about an hour past sunset, that enough time?"

"That will be adequate," I said. "I'm fairly certain he will see us before then."

"Right, if you piss off Pollux, this is going to get messy in a hurry."

"Duly noted," I said. "We'll speak soon."

He ended the call.

"RPGs?" I said, giving Tiger a look in incredulity. "Really?"

"What do you want him to bring?" she snapped, "flash-bangs? Please, that wouldn't frighten a child. They need to feel a real threat, not some simulated light show, full of sound and fury, but signifying nothing. No, less than nothing."

"RPGs will get us the worst possible response," I said, weaving my way through traffic. "We don't want collateral damage, just access to Fakul and the gauntlet."

"That's going to come at a price."

"I know," I said, heading across town. "Let's just hope the price is not too steep."

TWENTY-SIX

I reached One East 60th between Madison and Fifth Avenues and parked outside the Hybrid.

We had about an hour before sunset, which gave me enough time to have a meeting with Castor. I wasn't going to try and have a discussion with Pollux. That would be an exercise in futility.

Castor tended to be the more reasonable of the two siblings, though Pollux exerted a sizable influence on him. Castor could listen to reason, while Pollux would prefer to respond with his fists or a blade.

I stepped to the guardhouse and looked into the verification screen, which confirmed my identity. I informed the guard that Tiger was my plus one, and he let us through the formidable wrought iron fence.

The exterior of the property held a garden, complete with a large fountain and benches to enjoy an afternoon sitting in the relative silence. Currently, the garden was empty.

I made my way around the exterior path.

To either side of the path, I could see the oblivion circles, which covered most of the area to either side of the path.

This was certainly not a place to stray from the path. One misstep could cost you your life.

The actual structure, which used to house the Metropolitan Club, dated back to early New York and had been constructed with old money.

We went through the main entrance and stepped into the official lobby of the building. I personally knew of at least three other entrances, two which were difficult to locate, and one which was secret.

A building this old had plenty of secrets to divulge, not all of them good.

A grand double staircase led to an arcade on the second level, which overlooked a large reception area. I noticed they hadn't replaced the central Bokhara Persian rug since my last visit, but knowing Castor, it was about due for a change.

Spaced evenly around the rug were small clusters of wingbacks, grouped in twos and threes around small tables, providing islands of privacy for some of the less social guests.

The ornate wood ceiling was an impressive work of art that contained copious amounts of gold leaf and marble, giving the entire lobby a palatial feel. Opposite the grand staircase sat an extravagant fireplace, which held a substantial fire.

Everything about the Hybrid conveyed a sense of entitled elitism which was reflected in the majority of the guests who stayed here, most of whom were demigods.

Demigods were a particularly unique group. They weren't as powerful as gods, yet were significantly stronger than normal humans. It placed them in an awkward position. The majority of demigods I had interacted with in the past suffered from a severe case of identity crisis.

Too strong for humans, yet too weak for gods. It made most of them cruel, self-centered individuals, deserving of a thorough thrashing.

I made my way to the large desk which served the reception area. Behind the desk stood a young woman wearing a nametag that read 'Smith'. She glanced up as I approached, and smiled while gazing warily at my clothing.

It was possible Tiger had been right about my getting pounded earlier by Fakul's puppets. I glanced down at my clothing and realized it did look a little worse for wear.

I put on my best smile and approached nonetheless.

"Good evening," I said in my friendliest voice. "Would it be possible to arrange an audience with Castor?"

Her demeanor quickly shifted from friendly to suspicious.

"Mr. Castor is terribly busy," she said. "Do you have an appointment?"

Tiger seethed quietly beside me, but refrained from saying anything. Truly, a first. Realizing that Tiger was about three seconds away from sharing some choice words with the receptionist, I opted for the truth.

"Not exactly, but we have known each for quite some time," I said. "Please tell him Sebastian Treadwell is here to see him. It's of utmost importance."

"Of course it is," she said, brushing me off. "Could you please wait over in the seating area while I check his schedule?"

She pointed to some the chairs situated not too far away from the desk. I tried to catch her eye to inform her of the error she was committing, but judging from her demeanor and the way she immediately preoccupied herself with paperwork, she had dismissed my existence.

Tiger slowly approached the desk.

"Smith, is it?" Tiger said, keeping her voice light. "You're going to check Castor's schedule?"

"Yes, ma'am," Smith said, looking up and noticing Tiger. "As soon as Mr. Castor is free, he will see your friend."

"My friend doesn't like to wait," Tiger said. "Do you think you could do us a favor and call Mr. Castor now?"

"I'm afraid not," Smith said. "Company policy states that—"

Tiger stepped closer to the desk and lowered her voice.

"I know you're just brushing us off," Tiger said. "Castor has a standing No Visitors policy. He never sees anyone. Ever. So here's what you're going to do. Dial his office line. Now."

Smith had looked nervously to the side where one of the lobby security guards stood. She did not catch his attention, but was desperately hoping he would soon notice the duress she was under.

"I can't do that, ma'am," Smith said in a loud voice. "You don't have an appointment."

She coughed loudly, getting the guard's attention. He approached Tiger from the side. If he had known who he was approaching, he would have called for backup.

"What seems to be the trouble?" the guard asked. "Can I help you?"

"Ms.—I'm sorry I didn't quite catch your name—" Smith said. "They would like to see Mr. Castor."

The guard shook his head.

"I'm sorry," the guard said, giving Tiger a once-over and deeming her not much of a threat. I had seen this mistake repeated countless times. It was an easy mistake to make, at least until she unleashed that first fist. "Mr. Castor's schedule is packed. He isn't seeing anyone today or any other day. Have a good evening."

The guard pointed to the front door.

Before Tiger could react, I placed a hand on her shoulder and stepped close to her ear.

"Do *not* kill him," I said, keeping my voice low. "He's just doing his job. Just get Castor's attention. I'll do the rest."

Tiger nodded and reached out, grabbing the guard's arm.

She closed her hand around his forearm, and I saw him wince as she squeezed.

"You've been really helpful," Tiger said, her voice still light. "But you see"—a little harder squeeze—"I *really* need to speak to Castor. Tell her to call him now."

Several of the patrons around us stepped away silently. They didn't know what was happening exactly, but they knew enough to sense that Tiger was dangerous. She had a way of bringing out the fear in people.

"Brenda, call Castor," the guard said his voice strained. "Do...do it now."

"But—?" Smith began. "The policy?"

"Now, Brenda," the guard said, raising his voice. "Call him, now."

"Fine, but I'm not taking the blame for this," she said. "This one is all on you."

The guard nodded vigorously as Tiger kept her grip firm and smiled.

"Thank you," Tiger said, handing me the phone. "It's for you."

"Hello?" Castor said. "I thought I instructed the front desk I was in meetings all day."

"I'm sure you can squeeze me in, Castor," I said. "It has been a while."

"Treadwell," Castor said, quickly composing himself. "What a surprise. Is that Tiger with you?"

"Yes. I only need a few moments of your time," I said, looking up into the camera overlooking the front desk. "I promise to make it worth your while."

"Have the guard escort you to the private conference room," he said. "And tell Tiger not to break him. He's a valued member of my staff."

I glanced over at the now-sweating guard.

"Release him," I said to Tiger and then looked at the

guard. "Castor wants you to escort us to the private conference room."

Tiger let him go. The guard exhaled, grabbing his arm with his free hand and muttering several curses under his breath as he stared daggers at Tiger.

"How did you—?" he asked.

"I train hard," Tiger said, stepping aside to make room for the guard. "After you. Conference room?"

The guard nodded and led us away.

"Thank you for not breaking him," I said as we followed the guard. "That was an impressive display of restraint."

"I know, right?" she said. "I'm impressed with myself, actually."

TWENTY-SEVEN

The guard led us to the door of a small, private conference room.

I checked the time and saw we had about thirty minutes before Ox began creating a perceived threat. I had that long to convince Castor that giving up Fakul would be in the best interest of the Hybrid.

If he refused, we would have to improvise. Improvising with Tiger in proximity usually ended in violence and destruction, with dashes of maiming to add flavor.

I really did not want to improvise.

The guard walked away, giving Tiger a look, while still rubbing his arm. Tiger waved as he left us alone. I opened the door and stepped into the conference room.

It resembled the sitting room at the Cloisters, but this was no area of solace. Even though the furnishings provided a welcoming atmosphere, the space was utilitarian and designed for work, not comfort or rest.

Large, comfortable executive chairs were spaced around the room or next to small desks. The subdued interior lighting was offset by the natural light coming in through the large windows on either side of the room.

At one end of the room sat a large desk covered in papers and monitors. I knew for a fact that Castor had a proper office. That he was using this space as one mildly surprised me.

Castor stood and moved to the center of the floor when we came in, gracing us with a reserved smile.

"Let me do the talking," I said under my breath to Tiger who stood next to me. "Maybe we can do this without violence."

"Doubtful," she said in the same tone. "He's all yours."

She moved off to the side and sat in one of the comfortable chairs. I could see why he chose this room to double as his office. The walls were a rich mahogany; the desk and bookshelves were of the same wood. I noticed the books were filled with esoteric texts spanning several magical disciplines.

It was an impressive magical library.

The floor was covered with a Persian rug smaller than the one that adorned the lobby, but no less extravagant because of its size. The deep reds and browns of the rug matched the wood of the walls. The eye for detail in designing this room was evident in every corner.

It may not have been a room of solace, but it was Castor's office away from the stresses of the Hybrid. I happened to glance upward and saw the mural. The ceiling was covered in a large painting of a ship on the open ocean fighting a major storm. The detail was exquisite. The artist had captured the strained expressions and muscles of the men fighting for their lives to save the ship from the onslaught of waves.

"The Argo," Castor said. "One of the many times it was saved from venturing into danger. You would think people would recognize when they are entering a situation that's hazardous to their health." Another smile, this one laced with menace. "To what do I owe the pleasure of this visit? Can I get either of you anything, tea or coffee?"

Tiger declined with a headshake.

"A guest," I said, raising a finger. "I'd like one of your guests."

"I see," he said. "I'm afraid you're going to need to be a bit more specific. We have hundreds of guests staying at the Hybrid on any given day."

"I only need to see one."

"Tiger, still as lethal and beautiful as ever," he said, turning to look at her with a short bow. "Thank you for not breaking my security. It is always a pleasure to see you."

"I'm sure," she said, remaining seated and returning the bow with a slight nod of her head. "Where's your angry brother?"

"Pollux is away on Hybrid business," Castor said. "He should return within a few days. I'm sure I can address whatever requests you may have."

Castor was dressed in an immaculate black Armani suit with subtle, nearly indiscernible, runework elements. His gray hair was, as always, carefully cut and styled. He moved back to his desk and sat behind it.

"Now, tell me more about this guest," he said. "I will do my best to assist you—within reason, of course."

"Of course. This guest may be currently under the aegis of the Hybrid." I said, taking a seat. "I would need unfettered access to this guest, with your permission, of course."

"You know our policy regarding the privacy of our guests, Sebastian," he said, sitting back and staring at me. "It's not negotiable. I'm afraid I can't give you access to *any* of our guests. It would set a dangerous precedent."

"This guest is exploiting you and the Hybrid," I said, keeping my voice calm. "He is using your goodwill and more importantly the reputation of the Hybrid to escape the wrath of those he has wronged."

"That's a strong accusation," Castor said. "Do you have proof this guest is actually staying at the Hybrid? Do you have a name?"

I removed my glasses with the pretense of rubbing the bridge of my nose.

"Fakul Bijan," I said and peered at Castor. "Is he here?"

"I'm afraid I don't recall the name."

A lie.

I sighed and Tiger picked up on what I had discovered. Either I was getting entirely too predictable, or she knew me too well. It was most likely a combination of both.

My ability allowed for my sight to discern intent. When Castor answered me, it didn't tell me he'd blatantly lied, but revealed the intent behind his statement, which was to keep something from me.

The truth.

"Castor," I said. "As a member of the Hybrid myself—"

"You, more than most, understand I cannot comply with your request," he finished. "Where would the trust be if I acquiesced to this private audience with a guest?"

"Do you know what he is, what he has done?" I asked. "What he is doing?"

"Unspeakable acts of evil, I'm sure."

"And if he were, would you still protect him?"

He shot me a dark look and nodded.

"I think you must have confused the Hybrid with some other location," Castor said, his voice light, but his eyes deadly. "The Hybrid was created to protect those who have no protection from the Councils or the supposed authorities. You know this."

"Fakul has killed countless on the streets of this city. He tried to kill me."

"Is that supposed to be a valid argument?" he asked, glancing at Tiger. "Are you sitting there telling me your hands, the hands of your Directive, are bloodless?"

"No," I said after a moment. "He must be stopped because he presents a clear and present threat—"

"The same is whispered about you and the Treadwell Supernatural Directive," he countered, pointing a finger in my direction. "Are you aware there are still stories about Death's Dragon on the streets of this city, Sebastian?"

"That's not who I am, not anymore."

Castor shook his head, pressing his lips together in disapproval as he raised an eyebrow.

"You can lie to me, or to your Directive, but please don't lie to yourself," he said. "In that regard, be true. Own this. *You* are here because *you* deem this Fakul to be a threat. *You* believe he needs to be stopped, and so *you* have become judge, jury, and executioner. This is the truth."

"Yes, because individuals like *you*"—I looked around the conference room—"and places like the Hybrid, offer these individuals shelter. The Hybrid offers them protection and comfort, becoming complicit in their acts. If my hands are bloodied, yours are bloodied ten times over."

"Yes," Castor said with a slow nod, his hard gaze unwavering. "The difference between us lies in the fact that I have accepted my role in this world. Have you?"

"You know I have."

Castor nodded.

"There is no room for white knights in our world," he said. "There are no damsels in distress to rescue, only vipers waiting to strike."

"I have no illusions about who and what I am, Castor," I said, my voice hard. "I have demonstrated this more than once. If I must be the check and balance for Fakul, and those like him, those who would prey on the weak and defenseless, those who would exploit power and seek more, destroying all who stand in their path, then I, and *my Directive* will step into the role willingly. Unlike the Hybrid, unlike you and Pollux, they will receive no compassion, no protection, and no shelter from me. All I offer is death, not absolution."

"Is that supposed to convince me to violate the trust of my guests?"

"Trust," I said, with a nod. "That is certainly a valid point. The foundation of this esteemed institution is built on trust, wouldn't you say?"

"I would."

"Most of that trust resides upon the notion and reputation that within the walls of the Hybrid one is safe," I said. "Yes?"

"Because they are," Castor said, an edge in his voice. "The Hybrid holds sovereign enclave status. No authority has jurisdiction within our walls; it has been this way since its inception."

"That's the thing about reputations," I said. "They can be such...ephemeral things. They're so difficult to create, taking years, decades and longer, to nurture and craft."

"Your point?" Castor asked losing some of his patience. "Our reputation is solid. We protect our guests no matter what it takes, and have done so repeatedly in the past."

"I'm aware of the Hybrid's reputation," I answered. "As I was saying, reputations are difficult to construct, but quite easy to destroy." I glanced over at Tiger. "What was that saying? A lie can travel around the world before the truth....something?"

"A lie can travel around the world before the truth can get its boots on," she said, glancing out of one of the windows. "Many think it was Twain who said it, but the original creator of the quote was Swift back in 1710."

"Impressive," I said, nodding in her direction. "I didn't know that."

"I try," she said with a dismissive wave. "Now you know."

"How is that relevant to my allowing you access to one of my guests?" Castor asked. "Why should I violate our long-standing policy of discretion and privacy? For you?"

"Because if you don't, a new lie will be perpetuated tonight," I answered calmly. "One that will cause you incalculable harm."

"You think I haven't been attacked or slandered?" Cast scoffed. "Do your worst. Spread your worst fantasy. The answer is, and always will be, no."

"I won't be spreading this lie, your guests will," I said. "It will be quite devastating."

"As I said, do your worst," he answered defiantly. "There's nothing you can say that I haven't heard before. Honestly, Sebastian? You expect me to take you seriously when you come here with empty threats?"

He began arranging the papers on his desk, ignoring me.

"I never said *you* would be the target of the lie."

"Excuse me?" he said, staring at me again. "What do you mean?"

"It's fascinating when you consider it," I said. "Plant a small idea and let it germinate. Give it some time and ample room to grow. Before long, that small idea grows into a full-fledged belief, one that rages out of your control, given enough impetus."

"Speak plainly or get out of the Hybrid."

I had agitated him to the level of frustration I needed. If he had remained calm, this would never have worked. I needed him somewhat irrational, acting on emotion and perceived danger.

In that state of mind, he would take the necessary actions I required. He would grant me access to Fakul to keep the rest of his guests safe. More importantly, to preserve the reputation of the Hybrid, he would agree to a pact of non-interference, while I dealt with Fakul on club grounds.

I needed to weave this web loose, to allow him to step into it, and then pull it tight, once he was caught in a trap of his own hubris. I was running the risk that Pollux would cut his trip short and appear, in an attempt to eliminate me immediately.

I had a contingency plan for that as well.

It wasn't a good plan, but it was still in place.

"This would be a simple lie, really," I said. "Something almost insignificant at first."

"Would it be along the lines of, Sebastian Treadwell really enjoys the sound of his own voice?" Castor snapped. "No, that would be too close to the truth."

"Nothing too extravagant; I wouldn't have to say anything at all," I said with a small smile. "You know how actions speak louder than words."

"What is this grand, but simple idea?" he asked, deadpan, as he returned to his papers. "The anticipation is practically killing me, really. If you could get on with it, I am quite busy."

"The Hybrid is not safe."

"Preposterous. The Hybrid is completely safe... Oh, you wouldn't," he said, his head shooting up as his eyes widened, fixing me with a glare of death. "You didn't. Pollux will kill you and your Directive."

"He is certainly welcome to try."

As if on cue, the first RPG sailed into the side of the Hybrid, rocking the building with an explosion.

I cursed under my breath, but kept my face impassive.

"*That* doesn't sound safe to me," Tiger said with a small smile as she looked over in the direction of the explosion. "That sounds like a rocket-propelled grenade. The very opposite of safe. Imagine what the guests are going to think, what they may say to their acquaintances?"

"You did this?" Castor said, glaring at me. "You ordered this attack?"

"Your guest has enemies," I said. "Enemies that care little for the sovereign enclave status of the Hybrid. You can give him to me, or...we can sit here and do nothing. Your call. I think I'd like that coffee—does the offer still stand?"

Castor took a deep breath and exhaled slowly.

"I'm afraid my courtesy only extends to those individuals who don't fire munitions into my hotel," he said, seething. "Does it need to be stated that your membership to the Hybrid has, as of this moment, been rescinded?"

"You just did."

"Sebastian, you are a right bas—"

Two of the phones on his desk began to ring, in addition to the cellphone he carried in his jacket. He answered the two desk phones first, dealing with the emergency, allocating security personnel, and evacuating guests to safety while dispatching first responders to the location of the explosion.

He took the cellphone call last, staring at me as he spoke.

I knew who he was speaking to.

"Yes," Castor said. "He's right here in front of me. I'm looking directly at him. He wants a guest... Of course, I told him it was out of the question. No, he's been here the whole time, but I know he's involved somehow."

Another explosion rocked the building. This one was closer to our location and Tiger's eyes gleamed with suppressed amusement. I was convinced there was something dangerously wrong with her.

"If you somehow managed to get access to this guest," Castor asked, glaring daggers at me, "the attacks on the Hybrid would stop?"

"Unfettered access on Hybrid grounds, disabled interior

failsafes, and sixty minutes of immunity," I said. "That is my request. If you can fulfill that, I'm fairly certain the attacks on the Hybrid will cease."

"*Fairly* certain?"

"Nothing in life is guaranteed, but your options aren't looking promising at the moment," I said. "Give me Fakul, or I promise you Pollux will return to a crater in a few day's time." I raised my voice. "Hello, Pollux."

I heard the cursing in response through the phone.

Castor turned away and continued speaking.

"Killing him doesn't guarantee the safety of the Hybrid, besides Tiger is here with him," Castor said under his breath. "It would take too long, and wouldn't solve the problem of the bombardment."

More cursing in response.

"Understood," Castor said. "I will tell him."

He ended the call and stared hard at me.

I smiled in return.

"My brother would like to inform you that your request will be fulfilled," Castor said.

"That's very cooperative of him," I said. "I'm pleased we could resolve this without unnecessary violence."

"Also, that before he returns, you should notify your next of kin."

"I don't think they will be all that interested in his return," I said. "In fact, I can guarantee you most of my kin won't care."

"Because," Castor continued, undeterred, "your days on this Earth are numbered."

"Agreed," I said, getting to my feet. "But...I stopped counting long ago. Now, where is Fakul?"

"Lower level of the west wing, with a contingent of his people," Castor said. "I'd advise caution. It would be an utter tragedy if something were to happen, resulting in your untimely demise."

"Your concern is touching," I said, walking away. "The immunity?"

"You have one hour as soon as you step out of this office. Then the full force of my security will be unleashed on you and"—he glanced at Tiger—"your people."

"Fair enough," I said, heading to the door. "Tiger?"

"On my way," she said and paused as she passed Castor. "For your sake, you better hope we get this done in one hour."

"You should hope for the same."

Tiger smiled in reply as Castor began making more calls. He glanced up once as we left, the anger in his eyes a palpable thing, as the phones began to ring again.

TWENTY-EIGHT

We moved quickly once we left the private conference room.

"I can't believe he used the *RPGs*," I said as another explosion rocked the building. "I told him loud but minimal damage. Is he insane?"

"I *can't believe* he used the RPGs," Tiger said with a fist pump, barely masking her glee. "He is *insane*."

"This is not funny," I said, orienting myself as we stopped at an intersection of hallways. "Get him on the phone and make sure the call is secure."

She connected the call as we headed to the west side of the building. Did I think we could deal with Fakul in an hour? It didn't matter. It would take as long as it needed to take. The hour window was to buy us enough time to create an exit, without alerting the security personnel.

"Reign of Terror," Ox said when the line connected. "How can I help you?"

"You used the RPGs?"

"Best of both worlds actually," Ox said. "Those turn-of-the-century buildings are built solid, Boss. RPGs aren't doing much other than cosmetic damage. Nothing structural. Anything else would've just bounced off with little effect. Did they work?"

Tiger gave me an *I told you so* look.

"Incredibly well," I said. "We're headed to the target now."

"Need an assist?"

"No, you keep on *not* destroying the landmark building," I said, pinching the bridge of my nose. "This is going to cost a fortune to restore."

"We have to restore it?" Ox said. "Really?"

"It's either that, or deal with a homicidal Pollux when he returns," I said. "You have no idea how he feels about this place. He is irrationally territorial when it comes to the Hybrid. If we don't restore it, he will level the block the Church stands on—for starters."

"He'll level the Church as payback? Whoa, the man has issues."

"I didn't say the Church, he'll level the block—the *entire* block," I said. "As for his issues, you have no idea."

"I'll make sure to hit easy-to-repair sections of the building," Ox said. "How long until you engage the target?"

"We should arrive at his location in five to ten minutes," I said, pointing down a corridor and moving with Tiger. "We have a small window of immunity."

"You're saying Castor gave you a window of immunity after you attacked his hotel so you can go deal with one of his guests?" Ox said, incredulous. "Seriously?"

"I can be quite convincing when I need to be, plus the RPGs helped," I said. "Nothing matters more to Castor and Pollux than the reputation of the Hybrid, and right now you're firing rocket-propelled grenades into that reputation."

"How long is this window?"

I looked down at my watch.

"Fifty minutes, on my mark," I said as we kept moving west. "Mark."

"Received orders given, expect results," Ox said. "Egress point?"

"West wing, lower level," I said. "We'll need a diversion in the east wing to cover our exit."

"I'll relocate now," he said. "Collateral damage parameters?"

"Zero," I said, my voice firm. "You hit non-essential areas. I repeat, non-essential areas only."

"Roger, we'll go quiet for now, then I'll grab everyone's attention in fifty on the east side," he said. "You make sure you're off the property by then. I'd hate to have to come back and get you."

"Me too," I said. "Radio silence until exfil."

"Roger that," he said then paused. "Oh, almost forgot. Tiger, Rat asked me to get you this. Said it's from Goat."

"What?" Tiger asked. "What is it?"

"Hold your horses," he said. "Keep forgetting how to activate these crazy parcels Rat uses. What's wrong with regular packages?"

"Rat's parcels don't need to be hand delivered?" Tiger said. "What is Goat sending me?"

"I didn't open it, I'm just doing the delivering," Ox replied. "Said I had to be within half a mile for this one to work. Guess I'm close enough. There, that should do it. Did you get it?"

A gray teleportation circle formed on the floor, vanishing a few seconds later and leaving behind a small, rectangular black case in front of Tiger.

"I got it," she said.

"Good," Ox replied. "I'm going silent."

He ended the call.

Tiger picked up the case before we continued across the Hybrid. When she placed her hand on the case, it gave off a subtle orange glow before unlocking.

Inside the case was a pair of thin, almost transparent gloves. Tiger removed the gloves and smiled as she put them on. They faded from sight a moment later.

"Gloves?" I asked. "Rat felt it was important for you to have these gloves? Now? Is he concerned for your delicate hands?"

"Not gloves, claws," Tiger said, making a fist and whispering some words under her breath. "These are my transdermal claws. They work with my ability."

"Transdermal?" I said. "They're in your hands?"

"What did you expect?" she asked. "Actual claws to pop out of my hands? I'm not some comic book character—though, now that I think of it, actual claws would be excellent."

"Let's not," I said. "How strong are they?"

She swung an arm and cut through a stone column standing near us. The section she sliced through fell to the ground in four smaller sections.

"That strong," she said with disturbing smile. "I think I'm going to like my kinetic claws."

"Kinetic claws?" I said, impressed. "Has that ever been done before?"

"Goat says no," she said, making a fist. "These gloves will allow me to channel kinetic energy into claws, whenever I want."

"How long?"

"Don't know," she said, looking at her hands. "I really hope Heka did some work on them too."

"Wonderful," I said as we started moving again. "Try not to accidentally kill anyone with your completely untried, new weapons in an active hostile situation. Do you even know how to use those things?"

"I have the basics down," she said. "I promise not to stab or cut you. At least not on purpose."

"That's reassuring," I said with a headshake as we moved to a corner staircase. "Let's go. We still have some distance to cover to get to Fakul."

"West wing, lower level is on the other side of the Hybrid," she said as we crossed the large corridors. "How large of a contingent with Fakul are we factoring for?"

"I encountered twenty of his puppets on the street," I said as we turned a corner and headed down the long hallway that joined the two sides of the Hybrid. "He was able to exert control at what I could only assume was a fair distance."

"So at least twenty of these human puppet mages?"

"No," I said. "There are benefits to staying at the Hybrid, but there are definite downsides as well. Castor and Pollux would never allow Fakul to bring in a contingent of twenty mages, no matter how he tried. It's against Hybrid policy to bring in a personal group larger than three. Fakul would have to adhere to that rule, or be refused entrance."

"Smart," she said. "A group large enough to feel protected, but too small to pose a threat to the Hybrid."

"Or so they think," I said as we crossed over to the west side. "I think you present enough of a threat on your own."

"I'll take that as a compliment," she said. "You *did* mean it as a compliment, right?"

"Of course," I said, turning left at the next corridor as another RPG exploded in the distance. "Actually, between you and Ox, I think you two present more than a credible threat against the entire Hybrid."

"I told you RPGs were the weapon of choice," she said with a hint of malicious satisfaction. "Do we really have to fix this place after punching holes in it?"

"Yes, so I would appreciate less interior redecoration with your new kinetic claws," I said. "We break it, we fix it."

"That makes no sense," she said. "The Hybrid is a den of criminals, and we have to fix it?"

"Only if we want to keep breathing," I said. "Pollux is a demigod, not exactly a slouch in the devastation department, and relentless in his pursuit of revenge. All undesirable qualities in an opponent."

"Would he would really destroy the Church?" she asked, glancing back at the destroyed column. "We're barely scratching the Hybrid."

We turned at another intersection and then headed down a narrower corridor. The entrance to the west wing was at the end of our current hallway.

"Yes, he would really destroy it," I said, slowing down as I noticed the two Umbra mages blocking the path to the west wing. "And that would be him just getting warmed up. We don't want to face him on a good day. After this, he will be livid, which is why I wanted little damage."

Tiger cocked her head to one side, cracking her neck as she saw the two mages at the end of the corridor.

"Well, we can't unscramble this omelet," she said. "Let's do what we came here for and get the hell out."

Their energy signatures were significantly higher than the human puppets Fakul had used against me earlier. They may have been protecting Fakul, but they weren't puppets.

"These aren't puppets," I said, keeping my voice low as we approached. "They have a fairly high energy signature."

"Not higher than mine," she said. "You can sit this dance out."

"You've nothing to prove," I said with a frown, "at least not to me."

"I don't have to prove anything to *anyone*," she said, moving forward, "except me."

I stood still and let her approach the two mages.

"Just a reminder, we haven't got all night," I said, tapping my watch as she gave me a hard stare. "Call out if you need assistance."

"This won't take long," she said as the mages shifted to the center of the corridor, blocking her way.

TWENTY-NINE

Both mages were dressed identically in dark suits and cream shirts with dark ties. The suits were runed, but the runework was visibly shoddy and would prove ineffective against any major cast. I had to assume Fakul had just begun on his path to becoming a criminal mastermind.

He was about to learn the first lesson of leading a group.

Equip your people with the best gear, and you don't have to replace them. Substandard weapons and protective clothing will usually result in your people meeting an early and permanent retirement.

"Stop," the mage on the right said, raising a hand at Tiger. "This area is closed to guests. Turn around and go back the way you came."

I could sense the mage on the left spooling energy into his body.

"I must have gotten turned around," Tiger said, using her innocent and confused voice. "I'm completely lost."

"Yes, you are," Right mage said, his voice stern. "Where do you need to go?"

It was a smart ploy. While Right mage engaged her, Left

mage prepared for an attack. With anyone else, it would have been an effective strategy. With Tiger, it was just a matter of delaying the inevitable.

I let her have this because I knew what was coming.

These two were strong, but I could sense the energy signature just beyond the corridor. Fakul had kept his stronger mage by his side. This third and last mage was waiting for us there.

Fakul himself was too strong for Tiger—not that I would ever tell her that. I didn't enjoy pain to that degree, but I knew what he was doing. He was trying to wear us down before we faced him.

Like the puppets I encountered earlier, these mages were expendable to him, a means to an end and tools or weapons to be utilized.

In a way, I was doing the same thing, except Tiger relished battle. This is what she lived and was willing to die for. For her, it was all about the fight. There was a certain purity in conflict for her, which was why I would allow her these fights.

Facing Fakul would be a different conflict entirely. My prediction was that he would attempt to use the gauntlet on Tiger, stripping her of power and her life.

He would be conniving, using guile and subterfuge to destroy her. Combatting that was not her strength. As powerful as she was, she could be deceived into acting irrationally. Her greatest strength was also her strongest liability.

However, to me, Tiger was not expendable.

The first crack of bone brought me out of my thoughts. Right mage was cradling his hand as he tried to unleash a verbal cast. Tiger punched him in the throat, cutting the cast short. Right mage staggered back, gagging and struggling to breathe.

Left mage formed a red energy blade and slashed horizontally at Tiger's neck. She raised an arm, hardening it against the attack and blocking the blade with her forearm. The surprise was evident on his face as Tiger used her opposite hand to drive a fist into Left's chest, launching him across the corridor and smashing into the wall.

He hit the wall hard, bounced off and crumpled to the floor, unconscious. She looked down at the two mages and shook her head before tapping Right mage with a fist to the temple and sending him to join wherever Left mage was in the world of unconsciousness.

"This can't possibly be the A-team," she said as we kept going down the corridor. "Tell me that wasn't the A-team."

That corridor led to a large empty, circular room with one door, and an additional doorway leading to another corridor.

"It wasn't," I said, keeping my voice low as a figure stepped into the room from the passageway. "Those two were the warm-up; this is the fight."

Tiger sized up her opponent and gave him a short nod which he returned. He was dressed in a simple dark suit, black shirt and no tie.

This suit was properly runed.

"Still want me to sit this dance out?" I asked, realizing that the energy signature of the mage across the floor was on par with hers. However, she would interpret my assistance as an insult. If I tried to step in, she would break me, apply a generous amount of torture, and then break me some more, but I still had to ask. "Or do you have this?"

She gave me a feral smile in response without taking her eyes off the mage.

"If you step in, whatever I do to him will appear like nurturing care compared to what I do to you," she said, the hint of the ferocious smile still on her face. "Are we clear?"

"Absolutely. Don't get dead," I said, stepping back. "He's all yours."

"We're here for Fakul," Tiger said, staring at the mage.

"You can make this easy and hand him over. Walk away and you can live to die another day."

"I think," he paused, looking up to ceiling for a brief second, before refocusing on Tiger with a smile that matched her ferocity, "this is a good day to die, don't you think?"

"I do," she said, giving him a short nod. "Tiger."

"Asim," he said, placing a hand across his chest with a half bow. "It is my honor to face you in battle."

"Before we get to the bleeding," Tiger began, "one question. Why do you serve Fakul?"

"You are wondering if I am one of his puppets?"

"The thought has crossed my mind."

"My mind is my own, as is my will," Asim said. "I serve him because it is my duty and burden." He pushed up his sleeve, revealing a faintly glowing golden triangle on his wrist. Inside the triangle, I could see a symbol that designated his rank. "Do you know this symbol?"

The triangle belonged to the Order of Three.

"No," Tiger said. "Does this mean Fakul owns you or something?"

"The Order of Three," I said. "Your life has been sworn to Fakul to erase your debt. What did you do?"

"I killed the son of a powerful man," Asim said, still staring at Tiger. "I was given a choice. Bind myself to Fakul, or lose every member of my family. I have a large family whom I cherish deeply. The choice was a simple one."

"I see," Tiger said. "That is honorable, even if the man you serve is scum."

"And you? Why do you serve him?" Asim pointed at me with his chin. "Is he worthy of your service?"

"I do not *serve* him," she said without a hint of animosity. "We fight together so that men like Fakul understand there are consequences to their actions."

Asim glanced in my direction and I nodded to him, which he returned.

"Shall we, as you said, get to the bleeding?" Asim asked, the smile returning to his face as he refocused on Tiger. "Weapons?"

"Whatever you think you need to walk away from this."

"Very well," he said and placed his hands together in prayer fashion. As he slowly spread them apart, he formed a gleaming silver blade, glistening with bright blue runes. "This is Nur—the Divine Light. Fortunate and cursed are those who gaze upon her light. It is the most beautiful and the final thing they see before death."

He extended the sword to one side, and for the first time this evening, I was genuinely concerned. Asim knew what he was doing. I was about to step forward when Tiger looked in my direction, freezing me in my tracks.

I nodded and stepped back.

Whatever the outcome of this fight, it would happen on her terms. She stepped forward and outstretched her arms.

"I am Tiger," she said, her voice low and full of menace. "A weapon formed from pain, darkness, and death. All who commit acts of evil fear my name. They tremble in my presence, for they know I am the winnower, separating the impurity of their existence from this world. I am the final arbiter."

They stared at each other for a few seconds.

Then the world exploded.

THIRTY

Asim lunged forward.

He was masterful in his execution. There was no wasted motion. Everything about his attack was efficient and deadly.

Tiger sheathed her body in energy as she pivoted to the side at the last possible moment.

I didn't know if she could deflect Nur—that blade looked dangerous, and the runes on its surface appeared to have been created to enhance its ability to cut, very much like the runes on my kamikira.

She drove a fist into his side as he crossed her path.

Moving with the momentum of the blow, Asim rotated into the strike, deflecting the brunt of the impact and swinging his sword around, slashing at her head.

Tiger ducked under the slash and formed a cross-arm block to catch the kick aimed at her face. She shoved his leg back. Asim retracted his leg, bending forward as he did so, switching his sword from one hand to the other to execute a downward sword strike.

It was a graceful and lethal strike as he swung down,

intending to cleave Tiger in half starting at the top of her head. Tiger rolled to the side and swung a fist at his knee.

He brought down his sword and nearly removed her hand at the wrist, forcing her into a glancing blow, which still sent him stumbling back as he shook out his leg.

He formed a series of nine silver orbs and let them float around his body as he closed the distance again. Each of the blue, rune-covered orbs was around six inches in diameter. They glistened with silver light like his blade, and I realized where the Divine Light name came from.

These orbs weren't exactly weapons, but reflectors for the power the sword would unleash, blinding Asim's opponent, and creating a lethal opening for him.

Asim was looking to end this fight, and if Tiger looked into those orbs he would. She would be blinded long enough for a swordsman of his skill to exploit the opening and end her.

She would hate me for interfering, but I wasn't going to stand by and watch her get skewered by a trick. This was an effective strategy against a fighter like Tiger.

She was expecting to fight to the death in a straight fight, while Asim was going to blind her and plunge his sword into her chest. She just didn't know how to fight dirty enough.

Lucky for her, I did.

"Stop seeing with your eyes and expand," I said as they closed on each other. "Expand or die."

If she heard me, she gave no indication of it as she dodged a thrust and side-stepped a slash. Asim was pressuring her, trying to get her to make a mistake and charge him.

He wanted to close the distance and use his Divine Light strike. I assumed for it to be effective it needed to be a close-quarters attack. If she got that close and he blinded her, it was over.

I materialized my blades and waited.

I was not going to stand and watch her die before my eyes.

If she had understood my message she knew what to do.

Tiger's ability was kinetic. Aside from having the ability to punch you repeatedly from a distance, she had honed it to such a degree that she could use her ability to feel the space around her.

It was like feeling around an unfamiliar area with outstretched arms, except for Tiger, it was omnidirectional and worked better than radar. She could literally 'see' with her ability.

By expanding her kinetic sense, she could see all around her at once. It was part of what made her such a fearsome opponent. The only person I knew who ever managed to sneak up on Tiger was Master Yat, and that had only been during her training stage. Once she mastered expansion, as he called it, not even *he* could approach her without Tiger sensing him.

Asim closed the distance, and Tiger let him. I rose up on the balls of my feet, ready to traverse the floor in an instant if need be. Asim, with a gesture, caused the orbits of the orbs to spread out.

He was going in for his signature strike.

It was then that I realized this wasn't a close-quarters attack.

The orbs, now orbiting the room were slowly growing, reaching nearly a meter in diameter each. Now I understood why he had chosen this room. There was nowhere to hide in a circular room. The light from each of the orbs would simply reflect off each other, bouncing between them, causing maximum blindness.

It wasn't a flash attack.

Asim was going to fill the room with light, washing every-thing out. He would make it too bright to see, like staring into the sun. The end result would be the same—it would cause temporary blindness.

And in that moment, he would strike.

His sword began to glow as he slashed at Tiger's leg. She lifted the leg, and punched him across the jaw. He rolled with the punch and slashed at her other leg, cutting into the outside of her thigh.

Tiger grunted in pain as the room exploded in blinding blue light.

I shifted my vision to minimize the effects of the bright light. My ability wasn't designed for this kind of vision, but it allowed me to see what occurred next.

Asim stepped forward to deliver the killing blow. Tiger parried the lethal thrust to her midsection, driving a fist into Asim's chest. With a whisper, blood erupted from his chest and back.

He stumbled back several steps before collapsing. As he fell to his knees, the orbs around us faded and disappeared. His sword vanished a few seconds later.

"Now I understand the words," Asim said as he coughed up blood. "You can see without your eyes. Your vision is sharper than your claws."

"Yes," Tiger said as she knelt beside him. "It was an honor facing you in battle."

Asim reached up and grabbed Tiger's hand, clasping it in his.

"The honor was...was mine," he said between gasps. "You have relieved me of my burden. My family is now safe and I... now I can rest. Thank you."

His lifeless eyes stared into hers as I approached where she knelt.

"He was good," she said as she gently closed his eyes, then took my extended hand. "Better than good. You let me face him on my own; my gratitude."

"I figured you wouldn't appreciate my getting involved, what with your pride and all."

"You formed your blades, though," she said, giving me a slight glare. "Don't you dare lie, I sensed them."

"I did. I am only prepared to go so far," I said. "For the record, I will not apologize, but I will help you deal with this nasty cut. It doesn't seem to be closing."

"His blade, it was probably runed like your blades," she said. "Designed to cut everything."

"Good thing you didn't allow him to do worse."

"Your hint helped. Thank you for having my back."

"Always," I said as I gestured, sending flowing golden runes to her injury. She sat on the floor and leaned against a wall as I crouched down next to her. "That should help."

"It's not healing as fast as it should," she said, looking down at the wound. "Shit."

"You're going to need more help than I can offer."

She nodded.

"Don't think I'm going to be much use to you with Fakul," she said, looking down at her leg again. "This injury is going to seriously throw off my dance moves."

"You've danced enough for today," I said, gesturing again and forming a teleportation circle under her. "Ivory or Haven?"

"Actually? Ivory," she said. "I know I say her eyes are creepy, but she'll leave me alone. At Haven, they'll start prodding and running tests, and all I want right now is some peace and quiet."

"Done," I said. "I'll make sure Ivory knows you're coming, and to give you the infectious patient treatment."

"Say again?"

"You'll be quarantined and left alone."

"That sounds much better," she said with a lopsided grin,

then became serious. "How long before the Hybrid brings the hammer down?"

I looked down at my watch.

"We have about twenty-five minutes before all of the internal failsafes are activated and security is dispatched to terminate any and all intruders, meaning me, of course."

"Can you do it?"

"I have one more cast, and then yes, I will deal with Fakul."

"Good," she said groggily. The healing runes I had used would help her sleep to accelerate her natural healing. "Don't you dare die on me, or I swear I'll kill you."

"Rest up," I said, lowering my voice. "Ivory will set you right."

The circle under her flashed green and she disappeared.

"One more cast," I muttered to myself as I stood. "Then we can call it a night."

THIRTY-ONE

In times of peace, there were several casts prohibited inside a populated area like a city. Most of these casts were battlefield casts, designed to inflict maximum harm upon enemies, while preserving physical assets.

The void vortex was not one of these casts.

A void vortex, if left unchecked, would devour the city and everything in it. This made it a cast of mass destruction, banned at all times—war or peace—and considered inhumane, even by the standards of magical warfare.

These thoughts were present in my mind as I drew out the vortex isolator and cast a void vortex. It formed in the palm of my hand; they always started out as something so small and insignificant, and grew into monsters of destruction and devastation.

I placed the isolator over it, capturing the vortex within the pendant. If Heka was right—and I really hoped she was right—I had about an hour before the vortex destroyed the isolator, causing me to unleash unimaginable destruction on my city. I placed the best mask I knew over the isolator, and hoped it would hold long enough to get through this.

"One cataclysm at a time," I muttered to myself, placing the isolator under my shirt and heading to the door. "Time to end this."

I pushed open the door and hesitated a moment, allowing my eyes to adjust to the dimness of the room. Not that I needed it, but Fakul didn't have to know that. Every advantage, no matter how slight can tip the scales in your favor.

"Simon Treadwell, in the flesh," Fakul said. "That traitor Castor betrayed me? So much for the protection of the Hybrid."

"Fakul, I assume."

He was dressed similarly to Asim with a dark, runed suit and black shirt. I was beginning to wonder if that was going to be the Umbra look. If so, it was a little too on the nose. He was a fairly handsome young man, thin and tall, not overly fit, but healthy from the looks of things.

It really was hard to tell with mages. We had a tendency to live long lives, and with enough power we could alter our outward appearance with ease. What he couldn't hide was his energy signature.

It was significant but lopsided, then I understood why.

His energy signature was concentrated around one of his hands. At first that struck me as odd; then I saw why: He was wearing the Gauntlet of Mahkah.

At first glance, it didn't appear like much, but as I looked at it, I could sense the hunger. It called out to me, beckoning for power.

"You feel it, don't you?" he ran his opposite hand over the gauntlet's surface in a way that almost felt obscene. "It keeps me company."

"It's sentient?"

"No, but its presence is with me, always."

"I'm sure," I said, examining the gauntlet from a distance. The metal that made up the gauntlet shone with an inner light, and I could see the runes inscribed in its surface glow a deep red. That was the source of the power in this space. "How long have you been wearing it?"

"Long enough to know better than to trust Castor or his insane brother, Pollux. I knew they wouldn't protect me," he said. "Even when I explained my vision, they couldn't see it. Short-sighted idiots. All they think about is money. Money? Why crave the material when you can have endless power? I offered them power in my world and they refused me. They betrayed me to *you*?"

"To be fair, I didn't leave them much of a choice," I said, taking in the room. "If it's any consolation, Castor wasn't happy about it and only gave me an hour to end your life before he acted."

"How generous of him," Fakul scoffed. "I knew he would throw me to the dogs. He was envious of my ability, of my power, and my potential."

We were standing in another circular room. This one had been modified to act as a staging area for the gauntlet. Fakul stood in the center of a large amplification circle similar to the ones sects used for duels and training.

This space was an amalgam of work space, living quarters, and training area. I realized the amplification circle covered nearly the entire floor. Then the door slammed behind me. I glanced back to see it had disappeared, and to briefly examine the smooth stone wall.

"That was a nice touch," I said, tapping the wall. "You created and maintained an open, interdimensional portal."

"No one is coming to save you...ever."

"This isn't exactly the Hybrid, is it?" I said, looking around closer. "You've created some sort of pocket dimension? Inside the Hybrid?"

"This isn't *inside* the Hybrid," he said. "Those fools

couldn't find this place if I drew them a map and cast the activation myself. They're hopelessly incompetent."

"Where exactly are we then, if you don't mind sharing?"

"A dying man's last request. Of course," he said. "This is a void splice. Think of it as the space between dimensions. A little hiding place of my own creation."

"An interstice," I said, admiring the room. "This is fairly advanced for someone of your level."

"Someone of *my level?*"

"No offense meant," I said, raising a hand as I continued to examine the space. "I hardly expected a low-level mage like you to manage a dimensional space of such precision. I am honestly impressed."

"You arrogant piece of sh——"

"I know what *I* want," I said, cutting him off and angering him further. "What is it that *you* want? I have an idea what Umbra is, but why? Why do you need Umbra?"

"Umbra is a tool, and I am its master craftsman," he said. "Umbra will create the opportunity for me to end the Councils. With my puppets, I will topple their supposed order and establish a new magical age, a new magical community."

"With you as the leader of this new magical community?"

"I am the only one fit to govern. You must see this by now."

"I have been gifted with a particular ability to see, yes."

"I know, I did my research on you and the Treadwell Supernatural Directive," he said. "I even briefly considered inviting you into my new community as peers."

"I'm flattered."

"You should be, but then I saw you were unfit."

"How so?"

"You have this penchant for morality," he said. "You move in the shadows, but somehow feel you are above them. It would never work—you could never acquiesce to my demands, to my orders. In the end, you would rebel, inciting others to do the same, and I would be forced to drain you, ending your life."

"So we're just going to cut to the life-ending part and avoid all of the unpleasantness?"

"We're so much alike, Sebastian, but I'm a better version of you," he said, adjusting the gauntlet. "You should have let my puppets kill you on the street."

"I have an acute allergy to death."

"Funny," he said with a nod. "Humor is good. It will make your death easier. Goodbye, Sebastian."

He made a fist with his gauntleted hand and the room expanded as he sank into the floor, disappearing from sight. Several doorways formed in the walls around the room.

"This doesn't look good."

THIRTY-TWO

I should've known better than to expect a one-on-one fight.

He was a puppeteer, for goodness' sake. It should have been evident he would summon puppets to end me. As amazing as my vision could be, sometimes I was completely blind.

All of the puppets that now formed were copies of Fakul, unlike the human puppets he had used before. What I was facing were the typical puppets a mage of his class would use.

These puppets were closer to golems—unfeeling, mindless and usually inanimate killing machines—impervious to pain and single-minded of purpose.

I was currently looking at three of them.

Wonderful.

I formed my blades and jumped back, preventing a puppet's gauntleted fist from slamming into my chest. As I closed the distance to the one on my right, I felt the one on my left do the same to me. I shifted at the last second, letting it drive a fist into the right puppet, knocking it down. One down, two and three to go.

Two pulled his hand hand back and reached out to grab

me. Letting that happen would be a horrendous idea. Knowing Fakul, these puppets were likely imbued with supernatural strength. If one managed to get hold of me, I would be broken body parts.

A major hindrance to my escaping this place.

I slid back and puppet Three took a swipe at my head. I dodged back and then leapt in to remove its head with my blade. It recovered faster than I anticipated, driving a fist into my shoulder and numbing my arm.

The one on the floor struggled to get to its feet. I absorbed my blades and formed an orb, dropping it on its face and crushing its head. I took a step back, forming more orbs.

I had opted against orbs initially because this was Fakul's personal space. Sometimes these spaces didn't always obey rules of magic, which meant casting an orb could be the same as casting a bomb in my face.

Never pleasant, but I didn't have much of a choice. This time, taking the risk had paid off.

My blades were incredibly efficient against living beings, not so much against inanimate puppets. I unleashed a barrage of orbs around me. They punched into the puppets, reducing them to rubble in seconds.

"Impressive," Fakul said from a doorway, holding up a gauntleted hand. "I know what you want, Treadwell. You're going to have to kill me to get it."

He disappeared into the doorway.

I knew better than to give chase.

This room was the hub. Everything else was misdirection, and I had no desire to run aimlessly in a labyrinth of madness. One afternoon in Aria's Corridors of Chaos was enough to satisfy my curiosity for a lifetime.

No, the solution had to be in this room, I just had to find it.

The circle.

I looked down at the floor, examining the circle closely and remembering my lessons in circle construction with my uncle Dex. A smile crossed my lips reflexively as I thought about his words and brusque manner of speech.

"All circles have two patterns, one for creation and one for undoing. They're not always the same, but, even in the most advanced circle, these two patterns will dance with each other. They may not intersect, but they are close neighbors. Find one and you can find the other. You just need to know how to see."

I removed my glasses and looked at the circle again.

At first, I didn't see the pattern—everything was too intertwined, too connected. So I worked it backwards, not looking at the patterns, but rather the gaps in the patterns, the subtle areas where they didn't connect, or where there were variations.

Then I found it: the pattern of creation.

As far as circles went, this one wasn't overly complicated; Fakul had hidden the simplicity of the circle under layers of what appeared to be a complicated design, but was at its heart a simple repetitive pattern.

I followed the pattern until it led me to the same pattern traveling in reverse, again hidden but easy to see once you knew where to look.

The pattern of undoing.

I gestured and began activating the pattern of undoing. A runic shockwave rumbled through the space, followed by more, smaller tremors.

"That's bound to get some attention," I muttered as I continued the undoing.

I was fully aware that if I didn't have an exit planned by the time this circle was undone, I'd be trapped in this space with no way out. Well, not just me.

Fakul would be trapped in here with me.

I was fairly certain he wouldn't approve. Rather than run me a merry chase through a labyrinth of his making, he would come here.

Fakul had been sloppy.

In his desire to demonstrate his superiority, he had revealed his hand, and it was amateurish at best. I looked at the wall where I had entered and I saw the dim outline of the door portal back to the Hybrid.

That was the only exit.

If he wanted to get out of this space, he would have to come to me. I gestured again and set the undoing of the circle to continue without my constant coaxing.

There were several countdowns going on in my head.

Fakul wasn't nearly accomplished enough to create a pocket dimension with a temporal anomaly; I would have sensed the different flow of time from the moment I entered. So if time flowed naturally in this space, the countdown to the Hybrid, unleashing death on me was about fifteen minutes away.

The isolator on my chest had a good forty minutes before the end of everything.

I glanced down at the circle; the undoing would be done in about thirty minutes.

This was providing everything went to plan meaning, Castor honoring his word of one hour, nothing destroying the isolator around my neck, and the circle under my feet remaining intact for now.

I looked down at the circle slowly unraveling.

This would be a simple exchange: I would stop the undoing for the gauntlet. Surely Fakul would surrender the gauntlet to save his life. If not, he was more deranged than I had accounted for.

I sensed him rushing back to the hub.

He raced into the room and drove his gauntleted hand

into the center of the circle, destroying it and causing the immediate undoing of his dimension.

He was more deranged than I had accounted for.

His action threw me for a split second. It was enough for him to get close and grab my arm. There was no sense in trying to break his grip. The gauntlet enhanced his strength beyond what I could break.

"Can you create another void splice before this one falls apart...can you?"

"Welcome back," I said, looking down at the gauntlet around my arm. "How about we play a different game? I call this one, Armageddon."

"You stupid fool," he snapped. "You were undoing my circle."

"I needed to get your attention, and I wasn't about to chase after you."

"My attention? My attention?" he yelled. "If this circle collapses while we're still in here, we'll be trapped. There's no other way out."

I had to admire his dramatic chops. Even in the midst of impending destruction, he still had the presence of mind to lie. Not effectively, but it was close.

"What about that door to the Hybrid behind me?" I asked "I'm sure you could figure out a way to open it again."

He peered at the wall, narrowing his eyes as if looking for a door that wasn't there, and then he began to smile.

"It's too late for you," he said, grinning at me, the madness dancing in his eyes. "You're undoing my circle, but I'll undo you before this plane is gone."

"And then?"

"And then?" he snarled. "With your power, I'll create another plane. I'll make my way back to the Hybrid and have a few words with Castor before I end him."

"Seems like you've given this some thought," I said. "And me?"

"You? I'll leave what's left of you here with this plane. You can die together."

He whispered some words under his breath and began to siphon power. I initially felt the pull of the gauntlet, but then it found the power of the vortex isolator, bypassing me and feeding off the void vortex contained inside.

An interesting fact about void vortices: trying to drain them of power via a siphon usually had the inverse effect, causing them to increase in size and power.

My cousin had found that out the hard way.

The best way to destroy a void vortex? Use another void vortex to collapse it. It was as insane and dangerous as it sounded and not guaranteed to work. Which was why the accepted method was to use the second best way. What was the second best way to collapse a void vortex? Unleash it in a space devoid of energy.

A void space.

I looked down at the glow coming off the gauntlet.

The runes in the gauntlet had grown brighter, the intensity increasing until the gauntlet itself started turning red, hiding the runes from sight and giving off heat.

"Impossible," Fakul said under his breath. "Not even an Archmage possesses this much power."

"You're right," I said, glancing down at the circle. The dimension had a minute two on the outside. "Maybe the gauntlet is broken?"

He whispered another word, and the siphon increased in intensity.

"It's not broken," he said, exulting in the power coursing through his body. "I'm stronger now than any mage. I am a god!"

I formed one of my blades and whispered a word of my

own as I sliced down and through his forearm, cutting just above the gauntlet. The gauntlet was still attached to my bicep, but the siphon had stopped. I pushed back and away from him.

"No!" he screamed as he lunged for my throat. I tugged down on the isolator and thrust it into his outstretched hand, crushing it as I shoved him back. "Give it to me!"

"I just did," I said as the void vortex exploded into him. "Now you have the power of a god."

I saw the seam of the doorway leading back to the Hybrid and placed a hand on the wall. With my other hand, I formed a short distance teleportation circle, using elements of the circle Fakul had destroyed.

I didn't need to go far, I just needed to get out of this space. The void vortex had begun devouring the space. Fakul was caught in its power, his eyes closed as it slowly surrounded him.

Whatever he was experiencing, I wanted no part of it. Especially when he went from serene to screams as the vortex began undoing him.

I whispered a word of power and really hoped I had been paying attention when my uncle had taught me these words. If this didn't work, this was going to be one of my shortest casts.

The circle glowed a bright green and then disappeared...

I looked around the room and realized this scene would be the last thing I gazed upon.

"Bloody hell," I said. "Might as well get this over with."

I had taken a step forward toward the vortex, when my jacket was grabbed by the collar and I was yanked back into the Hybrid. The door disappeared as I landed on the floor and slid back, but the portal was still there, partially open.

"I told you I could find him," a familiar voice said. "I can find him *anywhere*."

"That's the only reason you're still breathing," Tiger said from behind me. "Ox, we got him, start the party. You plan on closing that?"

I felt a flow of energy closing and sealing the void space.

"Done," the familiar voice said. "You're welcome."

"Sure," Tiger said, extending a hand in my direction. "We need to get scarce."

A few seconds passed, and then explosions rocked the Hybrid. I turned to see who had found me and looked into the eyes of the only woman I ever loved.

Regina.

Things had just gone from bad to disastrous.

THIRTY-THREE

"Let's go," Tiger said, raising her voice and grabbing me by the arm with a look of disgust on her face. She was careful to avoid touching the gauntlet still attached to me. "Why is there a bloody gauntlet attached to your arm? Is that what's left of Fakul?"

"No, yes," I said, my mind muddled. "Why is she here?"

"Ask her," Tiger said, heading to a staircase that led to the lower levels. "We need to exfil. Castor reneged on your hour of immunity. What a surprise."

"Pollux probably had something to do with that," I said, turning to look at Regina. "What are you doing here?"

"They needed help locating you. I located you," she said matter-of-factly. "It's quite simple, actually."

"She was looking for that thing," Tiger said, pointing to the gauntlet as we descended. "I told her if she helped me find you, she would most likely find the gauntlet."

"Why aren't you at Ivory's Tower?" I asked, still somewhat confused. "She healed you?"

"Good as new," Tiger said, tapping her leg. "We lost you and nothing worked to find you, so..."

"You reached out to Regina?" I said, then glanced in Regina's direction. "Thank you for the assist."

"My pleasure," Regina said with a slight smile. "I'm going to need your assistance later; my motives weren't completely altruistic."

At the foot of the stairs we came to a large steel door.

Tiger raised a finger.

"One moment," Tiger said, tapping her ear. "We're at the door, blow it."

"Ten seconds," I heard Ox say. "Step back."

We moved back up the stairs and Ox blew the lock with a muffled explosion. He shoved the door open and motioned for us to come to him.

"Let's go people! We don't have all night!" he yelled, then pointed at my arm. "What the hell is that?"

"Don't touch it," I said, glancing at the gauntlet. "It's inert for now. Get us to Goat. I need to get this thing off of me."

We traversed underground passages behind Ox for nearly twenty minutes before he came to a stop and indicated a stairwell leading up. We arrived at the surface several blocks away from the Hybrid.

"That's our ride," Ox said, pointing to a large Consolidated Edison truck parked near an open manhole. Several men were working near the truck, with others climbing up and down a ladder. "Best hiding spot is in plain sight."

Another Con Ed truck sidled up to the first one, and Ox led us to the rear as the truck detached from the work crew, then he headed to the front to drive. The interior of the back was where the facade ended. I slumped in a small comfortable sofa, closing my eyes, and resting my head back.

"Is he dead?" Tiger asked her voice tight. "Did you end Fakul?"

I nodded.

"He was undone by a void vortex," I said. "He tried to

siphon my energy with this thing." I pointed to the gauntlet still attached to my arm. "But it latched on to the vortex instead. His end wasn't pretty, but it was deserved."

"A void vortex?" Regina asked surprised. "That was risky."

"A calculated one," I said, keeping my eyes closed. "It was the best way to combat the gauntlet."

"Did you collapse it?"

"No," I said, remembering the image of Fakul being undone, before opening my eyes. "I released the vortex in a void space. It devoured everything within the space, including Fakul."

"Good," Tiger said, sitting on another small sofa opposite from me. "That should end Umbra too."

"We'll make sure Umbra is disbanded. They should be weakened with Fakul gone," I said. "Have Rat track them down and dissuade them from any other Umbra-related activities."

"I'll let him know," Tiger said, glaring at Regina. "Tell her she can't have it."

"She knows she can't," I said, still admiring the ceiling of the truck. "Regina, why don't you tell her why you're here. I know it's not for this thing."

"You always knew me too well," Regina said, getting to her feet. "You know why I'm here, Seb. This is my stop, Ox."

The truck came to a stop and she moved to the rear door.

She turned at the door and looked at me. I did my best not to look back.

I lasted all of two seconds.

"You need to walk away," I said, gazing into her eyes. "Now, while you still can."

"It's always good to see you, Sebastian," she said. "You look good."

"They're not going to give it to you."

"I'm not asking," she said, smiling at me. "I'll see you soon, Seb."

"I really hope not," I said as she opened the door, dropped down onto the street, and walked away. "For your sake."

"What did she mean, she's not asking?" Tiger asked. "Why is she here if she isn't after that gross thing?"

"The amethyst—she's going to steal it."

"The amethyst?" Tiger asked, incredulous. "She's going to steal Heka's sacred amethyst?"

"At the very least, she's going to try."

"Are you going to stop her?" Tiger asked. "I hate to admit it, but she's an amazing thief. If we don't step in, she will definitely get the amethyst."

"We deal with one disaster at a time," I said, resting my head back after Tiger closed the door. "Right now, we still have Char to deal with. Let's go, Ox."

The truck moved slowly and then picked up speed.

We arrived at the Church sometime later, the truck coming to a slow stop. Ox pulled the back door open and led us to the rear of the Church. Tiger and I took the small stairs down into the rear entrance, walking through the catacombs until we arrived at Goat's lair.

The familiar sound of metal on metal was absent, replaced by low conversation as I pushed the large steel door open. I braced myself against the usual wall of heat as I peered into the forge, but that too was minimal.

The heat of the lair, which usually unbearable, was concentrated to one of the far forges on the floor. Several furnaces were still bright with flames, but most of them were empty.

I stood silently at the entrance with Tiger by my side.

Goat stood to one side of a large metal table, with Heka on the opposite side. They both wore rune-covered leather aprons. Their expressions were serious as they examined the large book in front of them. On another table close by rested the duplicate gauntlet they had created.

Every so often, one of them would point to one section of the gauntlet, which rested in the center of the table, and then refer back to the book. The other would then work on it with assistance from the one reading from the book.

They barely needed to speak, each one understanding the other intuitively. They made a good team.

"If we had the gauntlet, I could get a better angle on that side," Heka said. "It's nearly impossible to imagine which runes were used on the blind side."

"I think I can help with that," I said, stepping further into the forge and raising my voice. "Hello, Goat, Heka. Would one of you be gracious enough to remove this from my arm without using the retrieval method I favored?"

"Which was?" Heka asked. "How did you get it off his hand?"

"He didn't," Goat said, pointing at the gauntlet. "He removed the rest of the wielder."

"I see," Heka said, stepping close and examining the gauntlet. "Brutal, but effective. And you say you want to keep this arm?"

"I've grown attached to it, yes," I said, staring at her. "I'm sure your two great intellects can devise another method, one that doesn't require me to lose an arm."

They examined the gauntlet for about a minute. In the end, I had to sacrifice my jacket for the cause as they cut it away and managed to open the gauntlet wide enough to pry my arm out of its grip.

"I don't recommend wearing it, not even as a test," I said, removing the rest of my jacket and tossing it into one of the furnaces. "It has serious parasitic tendencies."

"I can feel the hunger from here," Heka said, shaking her

head. "Are you sure you don't want to destroy it now? This is a dangerous weapon."

"Can you mimic the properties?"

"With this?" she said, pointing to the gauntlet. "It's possible, yes. I can see all of the runes clearly now."

"How soon can you complete the duplicate?" I asked, glancing at the fake gauntlet on the other table. "Char will know about what happened at the Hybrid, if she doesn't know already."

"We'll need a few days," Goat said, holding the gauntlet with tongs. "We have the model ready; the difficult section was the runes. Heka can work on that now. Two days."

Heka nodded.

"Why do you want to mimic the properties?" Heka asked. "Do you intend to create parasitic weapons?"

"Absolutely not," I said. "I'm interested rather in the siphoning and imbuing aspects of this gauntlet."

"Understood," Heka said. "We're going to need some powerful weapons for a test run. These runes would destroy most weapons."

"I see. Will these do?" I said, producing my kamikira. "Tiger, your claws, please."

Tiger extended her hands, causing her gloves to materialize. She handed the gloves to Heka.

"They're certainly strong enough," Heka said, looking at my blades and the gloves. "I think they can withstand the runework."

"Good. I'll send more weapons of the same caliber after we determine if the process was successful," I said. "Thank you, both."

Goat dipped the gauntlet into one of the open forges.

"Won't that damage it?" I asked.

Goat shook his head and smiled.

"No, the heat is to burn away the organic material. This

gauntlet is too strong for a little flame like this to do anything," he said. "I'll call you when the work is complete."

"Please do," I said. "Tiger, we need to arrange a meet with Char. Tell her to lift Wei's ban on you. If you can't enter the club, then I'll pay her a visit once the ban is lifted."

"I'm sure she'll love hearing that."

"If she wants to see me, it's not happening without you by my side."

"Smart man," Tiger said with a nod. "See you upstairs."

She turned and left Goat's lair with a wave.

"This is powerful magic," Heka said. "Are you certain you want to do this? To a dragon?"

"I've seen what this gauntlet can do," I said. "I'm certain I don't have a choice."

"We have our tasks," Heka said, looking at Goat. "Do you wish to stay and learn more about the process?"

"As fascinating as that sounds, I think I'll go get some sleep," I said. "Facing Char will require I be at my sharpest."

"Good plan," Heka said. "It's never wise to face a dragon while tired."

"I'd say it's never wise to face a dragon, period."

"Good point," Goat said, removing the gauntlet from the flames. "Have a good rest. I'll make sure you're the third to know when we're done."

Heka nodded and began studying the real gauntlet.

I left them to their work in the forge.

THIRTY-FOUR

TWO DAYS LATER

Goat paid me a rare visit in my office.

Heka had come along with him.

He carried two cases, one in each hand, and placed them gently on my desk. Tiger, who had just arrived seconds earlier, gazed at the cases.

"Which one is the real one?" Tiger asked. "Can you tell?"

Heka and Goat both nodded simultaneously.

"You're here to test if I can," I said. "and by default, if Char will be able to."

"If she can tell," Goat said, "you're not leaving the Dungeon alive."

"Oh, he's leaving the Dungeon alive," Tiger said quietly from the side. "Char isn't going to kill him, not while I'm still breathing."

"I'm sure she realizes that, which is why she'd remove you first," I said, glancing at Tiger before turning to Goat. "These cases?"

"They contain the hunger," Heka said with a hint of pride.

"That was my idea. Are you ready to try and find the real gauntlet?"

"Do I have to try it on?" I asked warily. "I'd rather not, if that's the case."

"No, wearing it won't be necessary, just scan the energy signature," Heka said. "Then tell us which you think is the real one."

They opened both cases and revealed two identical gauntlets. I adjusted my glasses and used my normal sight, seeing nothing that would distinguish one from the other.

I focused and used my innersight.

An explosion of runic energy filled my vision, covering both gauntlets. Again, no clue as to which one was the true gauntlet. I took another breath, removed my glasses and focused, releasing my truesight.

Heka obscured my sight with her hand.

"Careful," she said. "You do not want to bond with this weapon. Gaze, but not too closely."

I nodded and looked peripherally at the gauntlets. The case on the left looked plain, producing a subdued energy signature at best. The case on the right blazed with red and black energy.

My disappointment was palpable.

They had failed to produce a viable duplicate.

I would have to devise another plan for my meet with Char. Perhaps I could tell her the gauntlet was destroyed in the void space by the vortex.

That would be difficult, if not impossible, to verify. The question was, would Char believe me? I released my true-sight, put my glasses back on, and turned to face them both.

Despite this failure, they had performed admirably. I had no doubt, that if it had been possible to pull this off, I was sitting before the only two people who could have made it happen.

"It was a good attempt," I said, the disappointment evident in my voice. "It would seem this task is just beyond us."

"You've made your choice, then?" Heka asked. "You know which is the true gauntlet?"

"Yes," I said with a nod and pointed to the case on the right. "That is the true gauntlet."

"You're certain?" Heka replied with a tone of dejection in her voice. "The right one?" She pointed to the case I indicated. "This one?"

"Yes, I'm sorry," I said. "I'm sure you tried your best. Perhaps there are some hidden techniques that have been lost to time?"

"Perhaps," Goat said with a slow nod. "Or perhaps, you're wrong?"

"What?" I said, surprised. "I know what I saw." I pointed to the left case. "That one barely registers as a magical artifact. While that one—"

"Is blazing with power," Goat finished. "Yes?"

"We managed to disable the runes," Heka said. "It was Goat who deciphered the runes accurately."

"I couldn't have done it without you," Goat replied with a rare smile in her direction. "You helped me figure it out."

"I'm all for a mutual admiration party, but how?" I said. "How did you manage it?"

"You want to explain it?" Heka asked, glancing at Goat. "Will he understand?"

"He sees, he will understand," Goat said. "Explain it to him."

Heka explained the process which steeped in runic manipulation, mixed with quantum metallurgy, and esoteric and ancient casting. After a few minutes, she smiled and stopped the explanation.

My dazed expression must have clued her in to the imminent demise of any functioning brain cells I had left. I only understood the most basic structure of what they had accomplished.

I shook my head in awe at what they had managed to achieve.

Goat closed the cases and placed another two cases on the desk. These two were much smaller. Both were sealed with specific runes—one for me and one for Tiger.

I opened the one intended for me and saw my karambits. The blades, which were now black, were covered in strange golden runes. I placed a hand over the blades and felt the pulsing energy flow into my hand. A second later, one of the blades was in my palm, surprising me.

"Proximity retrieval," Heka said. "I added that. I know they're meant for close-quarters, but you never know when you need to throw a weapon. Besides, you have two. You can throw one and still hold the other."

"That is unexpected and excellent," I said, absorbing both my blades. "They are still kamikira, yes?"

"Yes," Goat said. "We couldn't change that even if we wanted to, except now, they're channels for power."

"Not siphons?"

"Siphons only work in one direction," Heka said. "A channel can flow in both directions. You can siphon or impart energy. They were formidable before, but now, they are terrifyingly lethal." A smile crossed her lips. "Some of my best work is in those blades."

"Thank you," I said earnestly. "I take it that case is for—?"

"Me," Tiger said, taking the longer case. "My claws."

"Fundamentally, they are the same. Like Sebastian's blades, we couldn't alter them too much," Heka explained. "I did manage to adjust your claws to match your awareness. With your kinetic ability engaged, you can extend claws in every and any direction from your body. I call it the kinetic briar. I hope you don't mind."

"Kinetic briars is good, but too long. Let's just call them briars," Tiger said as a slow smile formed on her lips. "Are they channels too?"

Goat nodded.

"We added runes to make them work with your intention," he said. "As long as you're using your ability, the briars will respond to your intentions."

"Very nice," Tiger said, taking the gloves out of the case and putting them on. "I can see several uses for that."

I shook my head as the gloves disappeared into her skin.

"They will need testing," I said quickly, interpreting the look on her face as impending impaling for some unfortunate opponents in the training area. "Try not to go around impaling anyone just yet."

"No time like the present," she said smoothly. "We have a meeting with Char tonight, at the Dungeon."

"Of course we do," I said, dreading taking Tiger into the Dungeon with an angry Wei. "I take it she agreed to lift your ban?"

"I would imagine she's eager to get her hand on that gauntlet," Tiger said. "Who are we to disappoint her?"

"Do we have the location?"

"Downtown."

"Convenient."

"Isn't it though?"

"What will you do with the real gauntlet?" Heka asked. "I'm sure Aria would be willing—"

"No. If word gets out the Director of the Wordweavers is involved somehow, there are several factions that would assault the Cloisters in an effort to retrieve this artifact," I said, resting a hand on the left case. "I would not direct hostile forces against Aria or the Wordweavers."

"Who then?"

"For operational security, I must refrain from answering that question," I said, with a headshake. "Suffice to say, I have a safe place in mind."

"Very well," Heka said. "My work here is done; I should be getting back to the Order."

"Thank you for your assistance," I said. "Please extend my gratitude to Aria for your services."

"I will," she said, then glanced at Goat. "I still have some tools to pack before I leave."

"You should do that," Goat said, oblivious. "Have a good trip back."

"Why don't *you* help her pack her tools?" Tiger said. "Maybe lend her some to go?"

"That's a good idea, I have some excellent ones in mind," he said. "Do you want me to send them to you?"

"She's here *now*," Tiger said, shaking her head. "How about you go downstairs and pack them with her stuff?"

Goat nodded, leaving my office with Heka in tow. Heka smiled at Tiger and mouthed a thank you. I could still hear Goat expounding on the traits of his forge hammers as he returned to his lair.

"When it comes to Heka, he's as sharp as one of his hammers," Tiger said.

"I think he's much sharper than he lets on," I said. "Those two are made for each other."

"You ready for tonight?"

"I will be," I said. "Can you call Rat? I need a word."

"Operational security?"

"Always," I said. "I won't put you in unnecessary danger; you do enough of that on your own."

She laughed and headed out of the office.

"See you tonight."

THIRTY-FIVE

It was early evening when I parked the Tank in front of the Dungeon.

The hour meant that it would be empty of guests. Only staff and security would be on the premises if anything went sideways.

I was under no illusion that this would go smoothly since Tiger was sitting next to me. Her capacity to disrupt most situations into a violent outcome was uncanny.

We exited the Tank.

I gave Tiger the case holding the duplicate gauntlet.

The gray, nondescript double door stood beside the entrance to MOCA, the Museum of Chinese Americans. In front of this door, in their impeccable Midnight Blue Brioni suits, offset with cream colored shirts, stood two very unassuming, but dangerous individuals—Fuxi and Nuwa.

The Twins of Death.

Fuxi wore a silver tie and Nuwa wore a cravat of the same color. Nuwa wore her hair long, while Fuxi kept his short.

As I approached the door both gave me a short nod. I

placed a hand on the runes next to the entrance, which announced my presence to Char, as I bowed to the Twins.

"Is Lady Char available?" I asked after taking a step back.

"For you, always," Nuwa replied with a tight smile before returning the bow. "She has been notified of your arrival and is waiting downstairs."

"Lady Char is in, and expecting you," Fuxi said, focusing on Tiger. "Please observe the customs of *non-violence* within our home, and enjoy your visit to the Dungeon."

I nodded and stepped forward as the gray doors slid open, revealing a staircase leading down.

"Why did that feel like he was talking to me?" Tiger said, glancing up the stairs as we descended. "I didn't appreciate that."

"You felt it was addressed to you?"

"Yes, it didn't feel that way to you?"

"Maybe you feel that way because you have a habit of bringing violence to the Dungeon?" I said. "Just a thought."

"There was no need to be rude about it."

"No violence, or know pain."

"I know the rule."

"This time let's try something novel," I said. "For once, let's wait until we are actually attacked before unleashing the pain, hmm?"

"I make no promises," she said with a huff. "If they leave me alone, I'll do the same."

We took the stairs down.

As usual, the smell of citrus, lavender, and a hint of cinnamon was the first thing I noticed when we reached the foot of the stairs. The low sounds of jazz played, setting the ambience for the expected clientele of the evening.

The reception area lounge was devoid of the Beautiful People. Comfortable seating, large sofas, and oversized wing-backs around small tables all sat empty, awaiting guests.

In the large, oval-shaped bar, the bartender was prepping for the start of the evening to cater to the requests of the guests. At the center of the bar, in his usual spot, leaning casually against its side, stood Wu Wei, the head of security for the entire Dungeon.

He looked livid, but kept it under control.

"Hello, Wei," Tiger said as we approached the bar. She turned to the bartender. "Lemon water, please."

The bartender slid a glass in front of her, moments later.

"If you start anything," Wei said, his words short and hard, "I promise you, you will wake up in Haven wondering what the hell happened."

"I'm on my best behavior," Tiger said, releasing some energy. "Besides, in order to send me to Haven, you'd have to get close." I felt the extension of some briars, forcing Wei to take several steps back. "I'd strongly suggest against it."

She picked up her lemon water and headed across the room to take the stairs to the lower level.

"What in the actual fu—?"

"She'll behave," I said, my voice grim with an edge of menace. "On my word. If you leave her alone, *you* won't have to wake up in Haven."

Wei nodded wordlessly as I followed Tiger.

We both nodded to Bam-Bam as he made way, allowing us to use the staircase heading down to the lower level.

"Good to see you again, BB," Tiger said, lightly punching Bam-Bam in the arm. "You behave now."

Bam-Bam made a show of rubbing his arm, and laughed before nodding to Tiger.

These stairs were covered in runes.

I paused on the top step, and took a deep breath.

"Let's just give her the gauntlet and go home," Tiger said, aware of the fact that Char could probably see and hear us. "That was the deal, right?"

"Correct," I said. "Let's get this over with."

The smell shifted here as the scent transported me to an open forest full of trees with a gentle wind blowing. The faint scent wafted into my lungs with hints of vanilla, rose, and lilac, reminding me of cherry blossoms.

The purity of the scent was an unspoken testament to the depth of her power. She was subtly reminding all who entered into her lair: *I am stronger than you can even imagine. I am stronger than you.*

I refocused on the steps, making sure the runes etched into the stone were set to defense and not active offense. Even though Char had lifted the ban on Tiger, she wasn't beyond exerting her own form of justice.

As we descended, I observed each of the runes was defensive in nature. I breathed a little easier, knowing the defenses had been disabled. The realization that they could be enabled with a thought from Char lingered in the back of my mind.

We made it to the bottom of the stairs without incident and stepped toward the set of glowing runes at the threshold of the training area.

The annihilation runes around the circular training area were situated in the center of the training floor and were currently dormant. I paused in my approach and looked around, seeing Char sitting at the conference table in her bone white, ornately engraved seat, *inside* the negotiation area.

That's new.

We approached the negotiation area, walking through the training area, being careful to stay off the wooden floor designated for the actual training.

I kept my gaze relaxed and fixed on Char.

She was wearing a simple, black and white robe with her repeating white dragon in flight motif. Her long white hair was pulled back into a bun and held in place with several long, black hairpins.

As we entered the negotiation area, Char waved a hand, causing the plexan wall to become an opaque milky-white, blocking the view from the outside.

Tiger approached Char, bowed, and placed the case holding the gauntlet on the table in front of her. Char lightly rested a hand on the case and motioned for us to sit.

We both sat.

We made sure to take the chairs closest to her. I'd have really preferred to sit at the far end, but that would only prompt questions, which would lead to actions—and then we would be fighting for our lives, and losing.

It was safer to sit next to the dragon, than to have to avoid her claws.

Char looked from Tiger to me and smiled.

With a small nod and a gesture, she materialized three small cups of the ink she called coffee. Tiger and I had learned our lessons long ago, taking only a sip to avoid being disrespectful.

"Thank you for coming," Char said, opening the case and revealing the gauntlet. "The Gauntlet of Mahkah. This should have never been given to that fool."

"Agreed," I said, remaining calm. "His plan was grandiose, but his methods were murderous and barbaric."

"As is usually the case with those who propose a new world," she said, removing the gauntlet from the case. "Rare is the leader who will elevate others for the benefit of all. Every would-be leader only ever sees one candidate for the position."

"It's usually a candidate pool of one," I said as she slipped her hand into the gauntlet. "Lady Char, I don't think that is such a good—"

She smiled and raised a finger silencing me.

"You think the power of this gauntlet is enough to over-whelm me?" she asked, the smile still on her face. "My hunger dwarfs this insignificant glove made by men."

"I still think it's a bad idea."

"Your concern is touching, Bas," she said, "if not entirely authentic. Even if this *were* the true Gauntlet of Mahkah, it would pose no threat to me."

Tiger's face was unreadable, but I could sense her tense at Char's words. How I handled the next few seconds would determine if we left the Dungeon alive or as a memory.

"I am of the opinion that few things could pose a threat to you, Lady Char," I said, measuring my words carefully. "How long did you know?"

"So you admit this is a false gauntlet?"

"Yes, it is a false gauntlet," I said defiantly. "Did you expect any less?"

"Ha!" she said, slapping the table with her other hand and nearly cracking the marble with the force of her blow. "A dragon never apologizes, Bas. Had you answered differently, I would have slain you where you sat. Well done."

"Thank you, Lady Char," I said.

"But you lied to me," she said, her voice serious, "trying to pass off this...this thing as the real gauntlet." She gazed at the gauntlet on her hand and focused. It turned to dust a few moments later, blowing away from her hand. "For that, you must answer. What say you?"

"Whatever the consequence, I ask that it only be meted out to me," I said without taking my eyes off Char. "The Directive should be spared."

"Oh, you think so?"

"I do."

"Did you forge the fake?"

"No."

"Did you inscribe the rudimentary runes on its surface?"

"I did not."

"Did you procure the metal?"

"No."

"And when you were inextricably lost between dimensions," she glanced at Tiger, "did you rescue yourself?"

"No."

"And yet you desire to shoulder all of the consequence?"

"Yes, it is my right as the dragon of the Directive."

"Yes, yes it is," she said. "Very well, Bas, all of the consequences—"

"Wait," Tiger interrupted, risking her life. "Me too. I helped him. If he gets consequences, it's only fair I get some as well."

"This has nothing to do with fairness," I said under my breath, still focused on Char. "You don't know what you are asking."

"Do you speak for her?" Char asked, still looking at Tiger. "Is your word, hers?"

"I do not," I said. "Her mind is her own. Her word is her own. I only request—"

"No." Char stared at me. "You will not request. You will accept."

"I will."

She looked at Tiger.

"I will," Tiger said.

"Good," Char said, placing her hands palm up on the table. "Your hands are now my weapons to be used at my discretion."

We placed our hands in her hands.

She whispered some words under her breath, and her hands erupted in white flame. The flames held no heat, but the surge of energy that flowed from Char into my hand made it unbearable to hold on.

I tried to let go and failed.

After what seemed to be a lifetime of agony but was closer to ten seconds, she released our hands. On the backs of our hands, I saw her motif. A dragon in mid-flight glowed a soft white.

Tiger looked down in awe.

I felt the way she looked.

To bear the mark of a dragon, especially a dragon like Char, was unheard of. She had officially made us part of her family, part of her enclave. Everything she had, everything she owned was now accessible to us, and would in time belong to us.

My mind could not process what just happened, but the obvious smacked me in the face. I couldn't help myself and laughed.

Char smiled.

"It certainly took you long enough," she said. "You may want to explain it to her, though."

Tiger looked between us thoroughly confused.

"You never wanted the gauntlet," I said. "You were testing me."

"Not just you," Char said, glancing at the still confused Tiger. "Her too."

"You were testing us?"

"Yes," Char said. "That gauntlet is a Weapon of Sorrow. It's designed to corrupt and destroy whoever wields it. You felt its hunger?"

"I did."

"Once it is on your hand, taking it off becomes nearly impossible," she said. "I had to make certain you would not fall to its allure."

"And if we had?" Tiger said. "What if we had given into the temptation?"

"You would have never left my lair," Char said. "At least

not alive. Then, I would have had to pay the Librarian a visit to ensure its safekeeping."

"I've never had a dragon mark," Tiger said, looking at her hand. "What does it mean?"

"Bas will explain," Char said, looking at me. "Now, your woman has returned to sow chaos. You have to stop her."

"She's not my—"

Char raised a hand and cut off my words with a look. Tiger stifled a laugh, covering it with a cough.

"You can lie to yourself all you want," she said. "I think I've just proven that lying to me is futile and ill-advised."

I nodded.

"She wants to steal a sacred amethyst," I said. "A Word-weaver design."

"Do you intend on letting her do this?"

"No, it's too dangerous, and unstable."

"Then I suggest you stop wasting time with an old dragon, and prepare to confront her," Char said. "She's not getting this gem for a client."

"She's after power?"

"What has changed, Bas?" Char said. "This is her nature, her strength, and her downfall. Your choices will determine how this plays out. Now, go secure the gauntlet."

We stood to go but she pointed at Tiger.

"Not you," Char continued. "You let an amateur cut you?"

"He wasn't exactly an amateur, he had this incredible sword, Nur," Tiger said. "He was good."

"Then you must become better. Besides, I would like to see what these claws of yours can do," Char said. "You *will* stay and train."

"Train?"

"Yes, consider it character building," Char said and glanced at me. "You're still here, would you like to train as well?"

"Thank you for the kind offer, but I have a Librarian to go see."

"That you do," she said. "Use the rear exit."

"The rear exit?"

She pointed, and a door formed on the wall just outside the negotiation area. I looked at Tiger who mouthed: *Save Me.*

I gave her a short bow and she shot me a glare.

I used the door Char had created and found myself in front of the Dungeon.

Fuxi and Nuwa bowed to me, placing one hand across their hearts. I noticed Char's mark on the back of their hands. I returned the bow in the same fashion and jumped into the Tank, my brain still reeling from today's events.

I had one more stop to make.

THIRTY-SIX

Dragonflies in the Reeds was open twenty four hours a day.

I stepped into the small cafe open to the public. The staff of young mages who acted as the first line of defense for the Central Archive noticed me as soon as I stepped inside.

One of the staff nodded at me, and headed downstairs, leading me to a small supply area. He gave me another nod and headed out, leaving me alone in the small room. He then closed and locked the door behind him as he exited.

A section of the far wall slid to one side, revealing a short corridor.

The corridor was lined with defensive and offensive fail-safes. At the end of the corridor, I saw the door that led to Honor's office. This must have been some sort of shortcut, or Rahbi had been called away on Archive business.

"Don't take all day," Honor called out. "Get in here."

I walked the short corridor and found myself in Honor's office.

"That was new," I said, looking back to the now disappeared corridor. "What's that? The express feature?"

"Something like that," Honor said, still dressed in his mage casual clothing. "I've been expecting you."

"I've been getting a lot of that lately," I said. "I came back to return this." I handed him the book on the Gauntlet of Mahkah. "Thank you."

"Did it help?"

"It did," I said, sparing him that Char saw right though our attempt at duplication. "Did you get my package?"

" Yes. When you send me an artifact like that, I expect you to show up sooner or later," he said. "Thank you for making it sooner."

"Thank you for accepting it," I said. "I don't know if you can destroy it."

"I can't," he said. "It's not only an artifact, it has a vast historical significance."

"Honor, you can't let anyone study it, much less wear it."

"I'm not insane," he said, staring at me and narrowing his eyes. "You're different. What did you do?"

I raised my hand and showed him the dragon mark.

He grabbed my hand and examined the mark closely, turning my hand in several directions to get every angle.

"Do you know how rare this mark is?"

"Not really," I said, "but I'm sure you do."

"I do," he said. "Char's enclave is very small, less than twenty individuals. Those who bear her mark are considered Charkin. It's a mark of prestige and power. Do you feel different? Have you exhibited any new abilities?"

"Does patiently tolerating your losing your mind over this, count as a new ability?"

"Of course not," he said, taking the question seriously. "You've always—oh, ha ha. Hilarious. You're only acting like that because you don't know what it means."

"Right now, it means you keep that gauntlet safe and away

from everyone," I said, suddenly tired. "Char would crucify me if you lost it."

"Char wouldn't subscribe to some Roman form of torture," Honor said in typical Honor fashion. "She would probably just disintegrate you slowly, keeping you alive the whole time."

"What a pleasant thought," I said. "Can you create another express door to the Tank? I need to get to the Church. There are situations on the horizon that require my immediate attention."

"Are any of these situations named Regina?"

"What?" I asked, surprised. "What have you heard?"

"It's what I haven't heard," he said. "A fairly large and volatile group of mage assassins have gone dark. No word of their activity, no sight of their members. Just gone."

"This group have a name?"

"Maledicta," Honor said, his words chilling me. "It's as if they fell off the face of the earth."

"Do you have coffee?"

"What kind of question is that? I *always* have coffee."

"Better pour me some and get me an outside line to the Church," I said. "You and I have much to catch up on."

He nodded, placed a phone on the desk and headed to the door.

"Be right back. Death Wish as usual?"

"Heavy on the death, please."

"Will do; see you in five."

I placed a call to the Church and spoke to Rat, informing him of what I just learned, and asking him to deploy his people to gather more information. I let him know where Tiger was, and my anticipated return to the Church.

He relayed the information to the rest of the Directive and informed me he would uncover as much as he could about this group, Maledicta.

I hung up, gestured, and formed a comfortable chair, as Honor returned to his office, offering me a large mug.

He glanced at the chair and raised an eyebrow.

"You intend on staying long?"

"Long enough for you to brief me on what you know and what I don't," I said, sitting in the chair. "I don't intend on doing that on my feet." I raised the mug in his direction. "Thank you."

"My pleasure," Honor said, sitting behind his desk. "We have much to discuss, may as well get started."

The aroma of coffee caressed me for a few seconds, before punching me delicately in the taste buds as I took my first sip of the dark goodness.

It was going to be a long and informative night.

THE END

AUTHOR NOTES

Thank you for reading this story and jumping into the world of the Treadwell Supernatural Directive with me.

Disclaimer: The Author Notes are written at the very end of the writing process. Any typos or errors following this disclaimer are mine and mine alone.

Family.

Sometimes you lose the one you are born into whether by circumstance or choice, and sometimes you have to create one.

In the end, we all need a family.

Sebastian has done just that.

Even though he has a large (and powerful) family (which will be explored in later stories), he has chosen to create one around himself. The Treadwell Supernatural Directive is a collection of individuals, all incredibly different from each other, but bound together by the thread of found family.

THE STRAY DOGS is the first story in this planned trilogy (I've said those words before). Initially many of you requested more backstory about Sebastian and the Directive, but like Monty & Simon, we'll learn about them as the stories develop. Why is Tiger the way she is? What about Goat or Rat or any of the Directive? All of their stories get explored and revealed over time through their stories.

The next book, SHADOW QUEEN, introduces more of Regina and the dynamic between her and Sebastian. Will she implode the Directive? How strong is she? How far is Sebastian willing to go for the woman he loves? All great questions I can't answer yet, but will in the next book.

I do hope you enjoyed this story.

Even though Sebastian is related to Monty, according to readers, he has a tendency to be less grumpy and doesn't explode everything. That explosive grumpiness must be a Montague thing.

One of the insights into Sebastian and what makes him an outlier (aside from the fact that he prefers to dwell on the fringes of magical society) is that he has a tendency to try and solve things with his wits, instead of his fists. However, he's not afraid of getting his hands dirty if it means keeping the Directive safe or pursuing a case.

Tiger on the other hand...well, you know Tiger—slice first and if they survive, then ask questions. She was a great character to introduce and is an excellent counterpoint to Sebastian's calm and collected personality. She is volatile and violent, but like Sebastian, fiercely protective of those she calls family.

It will be interesting to see how she deals with Regina in the next story; they really do not like each other. It promises to be fun and dangerous.

I want to take this moment to express my appreciation to you for reading this story and much like the other non-M&S stories, allowing me the latitude of exploring a different kind of story. THE STRAY DOGS is closer in feel to the Night

Warden books than M&S, since it deals with darker topics and a world M&S do not venture into often.

It was a great experience being able to bring characters that are familiar (Wordweavers, Honor & Rahbi, etc.) and show a different side to who they are, and how they interact in the larger scheme of the city. We get to see the world of M&S from a different perspective and realize there is plenty of nuance.

Exploring these darker nooks and crannies is always great fun for me and allows me to take an adventure into the multi-faceted world of M&S, learning more each time I do.

I'll take a moment here to mention Char (what a great name for a dragon!). Some of you have asked why haven't M&S visited Char or at least had interactions with her. Char doesn't belong to the same world of M&S in the sense that she deals with what may considered the criminal magical community.

I'm certain she is aware of Monty & Simon, but she has no need (at least not yet) to speak or interact with them. There may be an opportunity for them to speak and deal with her, but it would be easier for them to do that through Sebastian. Now, if Char wanted to speak to the Terrible Trio, who is going to stop her? They do have some unsettled business with the dragon enclave. It's quite possible they will need to have a *conversation* with Char to resolve that situation...we'll see.

If you gotten this far—thank you. I appreciate you as a reader and a daring adventurer, jumping into these imaginings of my mind, and joining me as we step into these incredible stories and worlds.

You are amazing!

Thank you again for jumping into this story with me!

BITTEN PEACHES PUBLISHING

Thanks for Reading!

If you enjoyed this book, would you please **leave a review** at the site you purchased it from? It doesn't have to be long... just a line or two would be fantastic and it would really help me out.

Bitten Peaches Publishing offers more books and audiobooks

across various genres including: urban fantasy, science fiction, adventure, & mystery!

www.BittenPeachesPublishing.com

More books by Orlando A. Sanchez

Montague & Strong Detective Agency Novels

Tombyards & Butterflies•Full Moon Howl•Blood is Thicker•Silver Clouds Dirty Sky•Homecoming•Dragons & Demigods•Bullets & Blades•Hell Hath No Fury•Reaping Wind•The Golem•Dark Glass•Walking the

Razor•Requiem•Divine Intervention•Storm
Blood•Revenant•Blood Lessons•Broken Magic•Lost
Runes•Archmage

Montague & Strong Detective Agency Stories
No God is Safe•The Date•The War Mage•A Proper
Hellhound•The Perfect Cup•Saving Mr. K

Night Warden Novels
Wander•ShadowStrut•Nocturne Melody

Rule of the Council
Blood Ascension•Blood Betrayal•Blood Rule

The Warriors of the Way
The Karashihan•The Spiritual Warriors•The Ascendants•The
Fallen Warrior•The Warrior Ascendant•The Master Warrior

John Kane
The Deepest Cut•Blur

Sepia Blue
The Last Dance•Rise of the
Night•Sisters•Nightmare•Nameless•Demon

Chronicles of the Modern Mystics
The Dark Flame•A Dream of Ashes

The Treadwell Supernatural Directive
The Stray Dogs

Brew & Chew Adventures
Hellhound Blues

Bangers & Mash
Bangers & Mash

Tales of the Gatekeepers
Bullet Ballet•The Way of Bug•Blood Bond

Division 13
The Operative•The Magekiller

Blackjack Chronicles
The Dread Warlock

The Assassin's Apprentice
The Birth of Death

Gideon Shepherd Thrillers
Sheepdog

DAMNED
Aftermath

Nyxia White
They Bite•They Rend•They Kill

Iker the Cleaner
Iker the Unseen•Daystrider•Nightwalker

Stay up to date with new releases!
Shop www.orlandoasanchez.com for more books and
audiobooks!

CONTACT ME

To send me a message, email me at:
orlando@orlandoasanchez.com

Join our newsletter:
www.orlandoasanchez.com

Stay up to date with new releases and audiobooks!
Shop: www.orlandoasanchez.com

For more information on the M&S World...come join the
MoB Family on Facebook!
You can find us at:
Montague & Strong Case Files

Visit our online M&S World Swag Store located at:
Emandes

For exclusive stories...join our Patreon!
Patreon

If you enjoyed the book, **please leave a review**. Reviews help the book, and also help other readers find good stories to read.

THANK YOU!

ART SHREDDERS

I want to take a moment to extend a special thanks to the ART SHREDDERS.

No book is the work of one person. I am fortunate enough to have an amazing team of advance readers and shredders.

Thank you for giving of your time and keen eyes to provide notes, insights, answers to the questions, and corrections (dealing wonderfully with my extreme dreaded comma allergy). You help make every book and story go from good to great. Each and every one of you helped make this book fantastic, and I couldn't do this without each of you.

THANK YOU

ART SHREDDERS

Adam Goldstein, Amber, Amy Robertson, Anne Morando, Audrey Cienki, Avon Perry

Barbara Hamm, Bethany Showell, Beverly Collie

Cat, Chris Christman II

Diane Craig, Dolly Sanchez, Donna Young Hatridge
Hal Bass, Helen
Jasmine Breeden, Jasmine Davis, Jeanette Auer, Jen Cooper, Joy Kiili, Julie Peckett
Karen Hollyhead
Larry Diaz Tushman, Laura Tallman I
Malcolm Robertson, Marcia Campbell, Mari de Valerio, Maryelaine Eckerle-Foster, Melissa Miller, Michelle Blue
Paige Guido, Penny Campbell-Myhill
RC Battels, Rene Corrie
Sondra Massey, Stacey Stein, Susie Johnson
Tami Cowles, Ted Camer, Terri Adkisson
Vikki Brannagan
Wendy Schindler

PATREON SUPPORTERS

TO ALL THE PATRONS

I want to extend a special note of gratitude to all our Patreon Patrons.

Your generous support helps me to continue on this amazing adventure called 'being an author'.
I deeply and truly appreciate each of you for your selfless act of patronage.

You are all amazing beyond belief.

***

If you are not a patron, and would like to enjoy the exclusive stories available only to our members...join our Patreon!

Patreon

THANK YOU

Alisha Harper, Angela Tapping, Anne Morando, Anthony Hudson, Ashley Britt

Brenda French

Carl Skoll, Carrie O'Leary, Cat Inglis, Chad Bowden, Chris Christman, Cindy Deporter, Connie Cleary

Dan Fong, Davis Johnson, Diane Garcia, Diane Kassmann, Dorothy Phillips

Elizabeth Barbs, Enid Rodriguez, Eric Maldonato, Eve Bartlet, Ewan Mollison

Federica De Dominicis, Francis August Valanzola

Gail Ketcham Hermann, Gary McVicar, Geoff Siegel, Grace Gemeinhardt, Groove72

Heidi Wolfe

Ingrid Schijven

Jacob Anderson, Jannine Zerres, Jasmine Breeden, Jim Maguire, Jo Dungey, Joe Durham, John Fauver, Joy Kiili, Joy T, Just Jeanette

Kathy Ringo, Kimberly Curington, Krista Fox

Lisa Simpson

Malcolm Robertson, Mark Morgan, Mary Barzee, Mary Beth Wright, Marydot Pinto, Maureen McCallan, Mel Brown, Melissa Miller, Meri, Duncanson

Paige Guido, Patricia Pearson

Ralph Kroll, Renee Penn, Robert Walters

Sammy Dawkins, Sara M Branson, Sara N Morgan, Sarah Sofianos, Sassy Bear, Sonyia Roy, Stacey Stein, Susan Spry

Tami Cowles, Terri Adkisson, Tommy

Wanda Corder-Jones, Wendy Schindler

ACKNOWLEDGEMENTS

With each book, I realize that every time I learn something about this craft, it highlights so many things I still have to learn. Each book, each creative expression, has a large group of people behind it.

This book is no different.

Even though you see one name on the cover, it is with the knowledge that I am standing on the shoulders of the literary giants that informed my youth, and am supported by my generous readers who give of their time to jump into the adventures of my overactive imagination.

I would like to take a moment to express my most sincere thanks:

To Dolly: My wife and greatest support. You make all this possible each and every day. You keep me grounded when I get lost in the forest of ideas. Thank you for asking the right questions when needed, and listening intently when I go off on tangents. Thank you for who you are and the space you create—I love you.

To my Tribe: You are the reason I have stories to tell. You cannot possibly fathom how much and how deeply I love you all.

To Lee: Because you were the first audience I ever had. I love you, sis.

To the Logsdon Family: The words *thank you* are insufficient to describe the gratitude in my heart for each of you. JL, your support always demands I bring my best, my A-game, and produce the best story I can. Both you and Lorelei (my Uber Jeditor) and now, Audrey, are the reason I am where I am today. My thank you for the notes, challenges, corrections, advice, and laughter. Your patience is truly infinite. *Arigato-gozaimasu.*

To The Montague & Strong Case Files Group—AKA The MoB (Mages of Badassery): When I wrote T&B there were fifty-five members in The MoB. As of this release, there are nearly one thousand six hundred members in the MoB. I am honored to be able to call you my MoB Family. Thank you for being part of this group and M&S.

You make this possible. **THANK YOU.**

To the ever-vigilant PACK: You help make the MoB...the MoB. Keeping it a safe place for us to share and just...be. Thank you for your selfless vigilance. You truly are the Sentries of Sanity.

Chris Christman II: A real-life technomancer who makes the **MoBTV LIVEvents +Kaffeeklatsch** on YouTube amazing. Thank you for your tireless work and wisdom. Everything is connected...you totally rock!

To the WTA—The Incorrigibles: JL, Ben Z., Eric QK., S.S., and Noah.

They sound like a bunch of badass misfits, because they are. My exposure to the deranged and deviant brain trust you all represent helped me be the author I am today. I have officially gone to the *dark side* thanks to all of you. I humbly give you my thanks, and...it's all your fault.

To my fellow Indie Authors: I want to thank each of you for creating a space where authors can feel listened to, and encouraged to continue on this path. A rising tide lifts all the ships indeed.

To The English Advisory: Aaron, Penny, Carrie, Davina, and all of the UK MoB. For all things English...thank you.

To DEATH WISH COFFEE: This book (and every book I write) has been fueled by generous amounts of the only coffee on the planet (and in space) strong enough to power my very twisted imagination. Is there any other coffee that can compare? I think not. DEATH WISH—thank you!

To Deranged Doctor Design: Kim, Darja, Tanja, Jovana, and Milo (Designer Extraordinaire).

If you've seen the covers of my books and been amazed, you can thank the very talented and gifted creative team at DDD. They take the rough ideas I give them, and produce incredible covers that continue to surprise and amaze me. Each time, I find myself striving to write a story worthy of the covers they produce. DDD, you embody professionalism and creativity. Thank you for the great service and spectacular covers. **YOU GUYS RULE!**

To you, the reader: I was always taught to save the best for last. I write these stories for **you**. Thank you for jumping down the rabbit holes of *what if?* with me. You are the reason I write the stories I do.

You keep reading...I'll keep writing.

Thank you for your support and encouragement.

SPECIAL MENTIONS

To Dolly: my rock, anchor, and inspiration. Thank you...always.

Larry & Tammy—The WOUF: Because even when you aren't there...you're there.

Maryelaine Eckerle-Foster: For the murdered out '66 Lincoln Continental that became Sebastian's Tank.

Orlando A. Sanchez
www.orlandoasanchez.com

Orlando has been writing ever since his teens when he was immersed in creating scenarios for playing Dungeons and Dragons with his friends every weekend.

The worlds of his books are urban settings with a twist of the paranormal lurking just behind the scenes and with generous doses of magic, martial arts, and mayhem.

He currently resides in NYC with his wife and children.

Thanks for Reading
If you enjoyed this book, would you **please leave a review**
at the site you purchased it from? It doesn't have to be a book
report... just a line or two would be fantastic and it would
really help us out!

Printed in Great Britain
by Amazon

46407065R00169